THIRSTING FOR THE VAMPIRE

SEXY SLEEPY HOLLOW BOOK 3

MOLLY LIKOVICH

"Love is inferior to you. I told you, you are not of Humankind."

— NOSFERATU (2024)

AUTHOR'S NOTE

This novella takes place in the *Sexy Sleepy Hollow* universe. This is a completely fictional version of Sleepy Hollow, New York and should in no way be compared to the actual town and its residents.

This story also contains depictions of things that might be upsetting to some readers, including: light dubcon, violence, blood, and bloodplay. It is intended for readers 18+. Please proceed with caution.

WHAT'S HAPPENED SO FAR?

Riding The Headless Horseman (#1)

Local diviner witch Arletta Harrington is widely disliked by the town of Sleepy Hollow due to her abusive ex, Ethan, spreading lies that she practices dark magic. One Halloween night after doing a tarot reading for local herbalist witch Samantha Waverly Kos, Arletta went on a late night walk and was abducted by The Headless Horseman. The Horseman—Hesse—confided in Arletta that he was hanged for witchcraft and then his body was decapitated. In the afterlife the God of Death granted him the ability to ride into Sleepy Hollow every Samhain to bring vengeance to the town that wronged him in life. He and Arletta fell in love over the course of one night and Arletta returned to Sleepy Hollow to find his head. Samantha helped her uncover a hidden mass grave of witch trial victims and Arletta was able to deliver Hesse's head to him. She then chose to remain by his side in the Realm of The Dead.

Smashing Pumpkins (#1.5)

Arletta receives visions of Hesse's past and learns that when he was alive he was Ichabod Crane, but after so many years in the afterlife he had forgotten his real name. Hesse is visited by Death who demands he either sacrifice Arletta or his recently returned head. For Hesse, the choice is simple.

Romanced by The Headless Horseman (#1.75)

Death comes to collect Hesse's head once more, leaving him depressed. Arletta comforts him, telling him that she has always loved him and that they were always fated to fall in love. Hesse purposes to Arletta. The two make a pact to return to Sleepy Hollow and make a plan to kill the God of Death.

Getting With The Ghoul (#2)

Samantha Waverly Kos is severely depressed after living a traumatic life and then losing Arletta to the Realm of The Dead. Samantha climbs to the top of the Sleepy Hollow clock tower and intends to jump off, taking her own life, but a demon named Albatross (Al) stops her. Samantha is the first person in centuries who's been able to see him. He begins to follow her, falling in love with her, begging her to summon him so he can be at full power. Samantha confides in him that her half-brother, Peyton, used to sexually abuse her when they were children. She had concocted a potion to help her forget, but when Arletta left there was no one there to remind her to take it and the memories of her traumatic childhood have been plaguing her ever since. Albatross tells her to summon him so he can end her suffering. Samantha grants his wish. Then the two attend an annual Halloween party held by Samantha's boss, Matilda Sheridan, and there Al kills both Peyton and Arletta's abusive ex, Ethan. Matilda becomes obsessed with listening to true crime podcasts about the mysterious deaths of Peyton and Ethan, and the disappearance of Arletta. Matilda then reveals to Samantha that she, too, can see Al, and that she's a vampire. She tells Samantha that Sleepy Hollow is full of far more supernatural creatures than Samantha ever realized. On Halloween night, Arletta returns to Samantha with Hesse in tow and tells her of their plans to kill Death.

PLAYLIST

Abracadabra - Lady Gaga
Disease - Lady Gaga
DO YOU REMEMBER ME??? - emily jeffri
Don't Blame Me - Taylor Swift
Down Bad - Taylor Swift
Dream Woman - Suki Waterhouse
Felt Good About You - Gracie Abrams
The Feminine Urge - The Last Dinner Party
Holy - Zolita
Hot and Stupid - Beth McCarthy
Hurt Me Harder - Zolita
I Went Too Far - AURORA
My Lady of Mercy - The Last Dinner Party
Now or Never - Halsey
One Last Time - Ariana Grande
Panic Attacks in Paradise - Ashnikko
Shy Girl - Haute & Freddy
Sinner - The Last Dinner Party
Super Soaker - Ashnikko
Sympathy is a knife - Charli xcx

Talk talk - Charli xcx
Vampires - Ha Vay
vampire - Olivia Rodrigo
VERSE - emily jeffri
Villainous Thing - Shayfer James
Young and Beautiful - Lana Del Rey

A NIGHTMARE

As is the way with many stories, it starts with a scream.

The seer is too young yet to know what she truly is; the extent of her power. She knows that she sees things others don't. She knows that ghosts and goblins and things that go bump in the night are real, but she does not yet know what this means for her. Like all characters in a story, she has no way of knowing that she is in one, so she has no idea that the tale has begun.

But as the vampire sinks her teeth into the neck of the teenage seer (with so much life ahead of her) the seer has no idea in this blisteringly, blissfully painful moment, that this is not the end.

It is only the beginning.

PROLOGUE

L et it hereby be known that in Sleepy Hollow, monsters, Death, and Arletta Harrington are real.

"Are you a vampire?" the victim asks, her voice quivering.

"Fucking obviously."

Matilda sinks her teeth into the woman's neck. She clamps her hand down over her mouth (some sorority girl visiting her boyfriend for the weekend) as she drinks down her blood, practically tearing out the girl's throat.

She's so hungry. The pain does that to her. Rackets up her centuries old thirst to almost uncontrollable levels. She's sure other vampires who exhaled their final breath without spasms in their muscles and aches in their bones do not struggle with this endless agony the way she does. Pain flare induced bloodlust is a beast far worse than your everyday vampire. It's what makes Matilda Sheridan one of the most fearsome of her kind. During some of her worst nights, centuries earlier before she had learned how to better control herself, she would cut down anyone in her path. When her hunger pains overtook her no one was safe from her fangs: man, woman, mother, child, elderly, sickly, it didn't matter.

It still hardly matters to her.

It was easy to enthrall the girl when Matilda approached her at the pub earlier. She flashed her other-worldly smile as the college freshman was flashing the bartender her fake ID. They danced, they drank (Matilda taking stage sips of a cocktail), and then Matilda offered to walk her home. The vampire moved with such smooth speed that she had dragged the girl into the alley before she even had the chance to scream.

Matilda did get to savor the fear in the girl's eyes when she caught sight of Matilda's fangs.

Then the pain screamed at Matilda and it was time to feast.

What made her weak in the eyes of the living now makes her the stuff of nightmares among the undead.

Once she has her fill, the woman goes limp against her. Matilda steps back and lets the body slide to the ground, landing with a grotesque, squelching thud. Then she takes a handkerchief out of her skirt pocket and wipes the blood from her mouth.

"Quite the display."

Matilda turns her head to the entrance of the alleyway where a woman shrouded in shadows stands. Matilda knows that voice. Ghost or not, that woman will haunt the Hollow for all its days.

"Arletta Harrington," Matilda says. "As I live and don't breathe." Arletta smiles viciously, stepping out of the shad-ows. "Aren't you supposed to be dead?"

The witch sighs, smile faltering. "Always a pleasure to see you too, Matilda."

Matilda huffs. The witch hates her, has for some time

now. Arletta hates everyone who doesn't publicly scorn Ethan.

"What are you doing here?" Matilda asks.

Arletta walks past Matilda over to the entrance to The Underground and draws the sigil on the stones with her wand. Such an archaic tool to use, Matilda never sees Samantha or hardly any other witch use them these days, it's seen as something lesser witches do; those who can't easily channel their powers. Wands are for the wild and feral. Yet, annoying as Matilda might find her, she knows better than to underestimate Arletta Harrington.

Arletta steps back and waits for the door. It appears to the witch as an old, cherry oak door with a rounded top and gold filigree details etched into the wood, a rusted iron latch in place of a knob. Arletta opens it and walks through. Matilda follows her before the witch can slam the door in her face.

Arletta glances back at Matilda as she heads down the oil lamp lit Underground corridor.

"Don't you have somewhere to be?" the witch snaps.

"I'm curious to see where Death's maiden is headed."

Arletta stops in her tracks and whips around to face the vampire. "The Horseman isn't Death."

Matilda smirks. "Just a harbinger."

"Bold to have an accusatory tone when you just *ate* someone."

Matilda rolls her eyes. "I didn't eat her. I drained her."

Arletta glares at Matilda. "Talk to Melody Lakes lately?"

Matilda doesn't dignify that with a response.

Arletta narrows her eyes, refusing to let up on her pointless interrogation. "And what about Ethan and Peyton? Know anything about their deaths?"

Matilda laughs. "Didn't Samantha tell you about that? I

assume you're hiding out with her. Did you bring your headless lover with you or did he finally cast you out? You can be rather tiresome, you know."

Arletta glares at Matilda, the witch's fingers spark with angry magic. She raises her wand and casts a silent spell that sends the vampire flying backwards, crashing onto the cobblestones with a huff.

"If you know what's good for you," Arletta keeps her wand raised, "you'll stop following me."

With that she rounds the corner and vanishes into the night. Matilda's joints scream. She apparently didn't drink enough blood to quell the flare. She growls, fangs sharp against her gums, rage radiating from every bone in her body.

Oh, how she wishes Arletta Harrington really was dead.

SPOOK STREET PODCAST EP. 19: DULLAHANS &
WHERE THEY LURK (transcript excerpt)

OCTAVIA:
Dullahans originate in Irish folklore which
makes it interesting that the most well
known one in fiction is the Headless
Horseman from Sleepy Hollow, since the book
that most prominently features him is 'The
Legend of Sleepy Hollow' by Washington
Irving.

ROSE:
Why is that interesting? Maybe Irving was
Irish.

OCTAVIA:
Would you let me finish? No, he wasn't. He
was American.

ROSE:
Americans can be of Irish descent.

OCTAVIA:
Would you please focus? The reason it's
interesting is that in the book the
Horseman is often described as the Hessian
Rider of the Hollow and Hessians were
German soldiers.

ROSE:
Is there no folklore about German headless
horsemen?

OCTAVIA:
No, there is. In German folklore they were
usually less aggressive and were meant to
catch criminals and warn hunters.

ROSE:
What do the Irish ones do?

OCTAVIA:
They were seen as omens of doom, coming to
collect the souls of those who were on
Death's door. Some also believed they
possessed the spirit of the Celtic God,
Crom Dubh.

ROSE:
What was this Crom guy's deal?

OCTAVIA:
He was a dick.

I CAN SEE THINGS YOUR PEOPLE CAN'T

OCTAVIA

There is a vampire in the bookstore.

She's tall with pale skin several shades lighter than mine. She has piercing blue-gray eyes and shoulder length black hair. She's lazing behind the cash register, dressed like she just stepped off the set of *Practical Magic*. She's reading a book, I tilt my head slightly to read the cover: *Wuthering Heights*. I wonder if she was alive when it was written. I glance over at my sister and co-host, Rose. Rose is completely human, nothing paranormal about her. When we were children I used to try and see if she saw fairies in the garden like I did, or heard witches' laughter in the night, but whenever I probed it was clear she thought we were just playing make believe.

From the extensive research I've done on the topic, people like me are rare.

Seers.

Mediums.

Woo woo hippies.

Whatever.

I've never met a magical creature I couldn't identify. There's always something about their aura or skin or eyes or *energy* that weaves itself together into a language only I, and other seers, can read. It only takes one cursory glance at the woman behind the counter in The Raven's Feather to know she's a vampire. Her fangs aren't out, but there's a slight glint to her teeth that even the richest celebrity with the most expensive veneers and whitening regimens could never replicate. Her hair falls around her shoulders with an unnatural bounce. And her skin—there's this glow to it that I know Rose and other humans like her can't see. I wonder if the witches in Sleepy Hollow know there's a vampire in their midst. I've seen my fair share of paranormal beings in my life, never getting the chance to truly befriend one, but Ma always made it sound like witches and vampires hated each other. Maybe she was an expert or maybe she just read a lot of Deborah Harkness novels.

Ma isn't paranormal and she can't *see* the paranormal like I can. But she always believed me whenever I came to her raving about ghosts and ghouls and things that go bump in the night. Ma was honestly more surprised when I came out as a lesbian than when I came out as a seer. It took her well over a year to stop saying things like 'you'll meet a nice man one day' and 'are you absolutely sure?' Looking at the vampire before me I'm *absolutely* sure.

"Do you think that's her?" Rose whispers, leaning close. "Samantha Waverly Kos?"

I know it's not because Samantha is an herbalist witch, best friend of the supposedly late Arletta Harrington (another witch and much more powerful according to all the online forums about local paranormal beings). A witch is harder to suss out in a public space because everything about them appears completely human, they just have the slightest dark energy around them that sometimes reeks of their magic. Each witch's magic has a different scent. Usually something earthy and tinged with smoke. The witch we ran into at the bus stop smelled of lilacs, honey, and a forest fire.

Samantha's magical scent is so strong (apples, graveyard dirt, and brimstone) it's exceedingly obvious to me that she's in this store somewhere. I can feel another energy twisted around hers, much darker than even a sorceress witch's power. This entire bookshop is rife with the most confusing magical energy I've ever felt.

I take out my phone and pull up Samantha's Instagram. I study the first photo of the witch then shake my head at Rose to confirm that the vampire before us isn't the girl we're looking for.

In the photo Samantha's sitting on top of her mother's grave, smiling softly at something off camera as rain pours down around her. By her side a candle burns bright, unaffected by the storm. She has her comments turned off. I'm sure most are about how good her photo editing is.

Samantha has darker skin than the vampire before us, and shorter, curlier hair. Whereas the vampire cashier is more of a whimsigoth, Samantha's photos all show her sporting funeral appropriate dresses that practically mimic the Victorian era with a 90's grunge flair. Her smile is strained in almost every picture except the one where she's sitting on the grave, eyes locked onto some mysterious figure behind the lens.

The vampire turns a page in her book. Unbothered. I can tell she knows Rose and I are here, but she's not going to acknowledge us until we come fully into the store instead of lurking in the doorway.

I can't very well tell Rose right now that we're in the presence of a formidable supernatural being, she might be deterred from proceeding further and we *need* a hit episode if we don't want our network to drop us.

"Let's go," I say to her.

I put my phone back in my pocket, Rose leans on her cane, and I ignore how my spike in anxiety is making my face burn, my cheeks surely tomato red by now. We head closer to the counter where the vampire waits, our equipment bags banging against our hips as we walk side by side. I offered to carry Rose's, she refused. I suggested she use her rolling walker instead of her cane since we had a lot of walking planned today, she refused that as well. I glance at her knees, knowing that beneath her jeans they're wrapped in compression sleeves, and take in the strained look in her eyes. She's so stubborn, like she's always trying to prove that she's stronger than her pain.

She is.

I wish she saw that there's nothing to prove.

"Hi." I rest my elbows on the counter to hide my shaking hands, plaster on my rehearsed smile, and pitch my voice a few octaves higher. Rose used to call me out for doing these things, telling me to just be my authentic self, but my authentic self is so riddled with anxiety it's practically debilitating. If I don't use this fake smile and voice I'm afraid I'll projectile vomit across the counter or pick my fingernails until they bleed. Dealer's choice.

The vampire looks up from her book and smiles. My world stops and I briefly forget what breathing is. Vampires are unnaturally beautiful beings, everyone knows this, even people who don't believe that they exist. But I've never actually *seen* a vampire in person before and now that I'm looking into the eyes of one I don't know how I can ever lust after a human woman again. How could any mortal bedmate compare to this beauty before me?

Oh, damnit. She's enthralling me.

I twitch my fingers and wiggle my toes to free myself from the vampire's mental grasp. Her gaze flickers in surprise at how easily I've broken free of her influence. Another perk of being a seer (not that there are many to begin with), in my opinion, is the ability to realize when any kind of supernatural being is enacting their powers over you. While some powers are too hard to expel (namely witches' work), the vampire's thrall is easy enough to free despite my never having faced the sensation before. Maybe I'm just that good or maybe the vampire wasn't trying that hard. For a brief moment I almost miss the feeling of her influence. Vampire lore says that when you're being lured by a vampire you can't feel any emotion they don't want you to, which means no anxiety. I've always wondered which pieces of vampire lore are true and which are just myths. I make a mental note:

Vampire thrall powers: real.

"I'm Octavia Majestic and this is my sister Rose." I press on, not wanting to let my freshly returned anxious state overcome me. I really should have let Rose do the talking, but it's too late now, my gay panic has spurred on my nervous rambling. "We're the co-hosts of the *Spook Street Podcast.*"

The vampire laughs. "That's a new one. Paranormal I take it?"

"Are you a podcast fan?" Rose steps in, taking the reins (she must be able to see my body tensing up. I wonder if there's a flashing neon sign above my head that reads ANXIOUS BITCH).

The vampire smirks again before pursing her lips together.

"Matilda is a podcast junkie." Another voice chimes in.

The vampire, Matilda, raises her brows. I look to the aisle off to the side of the counter where none other than Samantha Waverly Kos has appeared with a demon in tow behind her. Rose follows my gaze. She taps her cane against my shoe in excitement.

"You two are podcasters?" Samantha asks. There's an edge to her voice that I don't appreciate. She sounds accusatory, like a cop questioning us beneath a glaring lightbulb.

"We are," I say, turning to face her, sliding my arms off the counter and clasping them in front of me. I force myself to exhale and inhale and fight like hell not to overthink if I'm breathing too fast and if it looks weird and everyone can notice and is silently judging. "I'm Octavia and this is my sister and co-host Rose. We're from the *Spook Street Podcast*. We're here to investigate—"

"Arletta Harrington." Samantha's voice drips with annoyance.

I feel something sticky on my hand. I glance down and see I've been picking at my nail bed without realizing it. An angry bead of red bubbles up from the skin around my cuticle. I look quickly at Matilda, but she doesn't seem to register the blood.

Vampires immediately going into a blood frenzy like sharks when there's blood in the water: false.

The demon beside Samantha laughs. My eyes snap to

his, it only takes a moment for him to realize what I am. He leans down from where he towers over the tiny herbalist and purposely whispers loud enough for me to hear.

"The short one can see me, babes."

Samantha turns her neck quickly to meet the demon's gaze before directing her attention back to me. I do my best not to look at him, but it's too late, Samantha is scrutinizing me.

She doesn't trust me.

I glance at Rose, my eyes screaming *ABORT*! The mission is a failure, we must abandon ship.

"We're not just here to investigate the disappearance of Arletta Harrington," Rose says, ignoring me. "But also the mysterious deaths of Arletta's ex, Ethan Steen, and your brother Peyton Kos."

"Oh shit," the demon mutters. "A pair of idiots, these two."

This is bad. This is *really* bad. A witch with a demon tied to her is more dangerous than I think I can handle. Then again, I don't think I can handle a vampire either (in bed or elsewhere, regardless of what my libido is trying to tell me right now). The Raven's Quill has turned out to be a den of paranormal vipers and my little sister has no idea. She is, however, most likely aware of how close I am to throwing up so I really think we should move this along.

"Arletta isn't missing," Samantha snaps. "She's dead. I would know. I visit her grave and I live in her house. The one she left to me in her *will*."

The demon puts a hand on Samantha's shoulder in a manner that almost implies he's trying to comfort her. A weird thing for a soulless pet to do for the master that's entrapped them. But Samantha shakes off the demon's hand and steps closer to Rose.

"And as for Ethan, he was a piece of shit who beat Arletta. The world's better off with one less abuser in it, who cares why he was killed? Not me."

"What about Peyton?" Rose leans on her cane, tilting her head back to meet the witch's gaze. My sister is undaunted. "He was your brother."

"I'm glad he's dead."

The demon shakes his head. Matilda whistles low and picks up her book.

"You two are here to beg me to do an interview with you, right?" Samantha asks.

I glance at Matilda, but she's clearly not going to participate in this conversation.

"Yes, that's right," Rose says.

Samantha scoffs. "Well, that's too bad."

She turns and heads off back deeper into the stacks. The demon stays behind for a moment and despite my best efforts he ends up pulling my gaze to his.

"Don't think I don't know your secret, little seer."

He dissolves into the air. I glance back at Matilda, but she's re-engrossed in her book without a care for the two spurned podcasters before her.

Then daylight begins to glimmer.

I move back to the counter, anxiety be damned. "Are you Matilda Sheridan?"

Matilda looks up from her book and smirks. It's lascivious and dastardly and so fucking sexy it could undo me without any vampiric enthrallment at all.

"Are you going to ask if I'll give you the exclusive tell all about why those two dumb boys my employee hates so much were gutted at my Halloween party a month ago?"

"I...uh...well, yes."

Wow, Via, how eloquent and verbose of you.

Matilda laughs louder than before. "Dearie, I don't know where you came from—"

"We're from Maryland," Rose cuts in.

Matilda ignores her and continues on as if my sister never spoke. "—or what you really hope to accomplish here, but let's get one thing straight: no one comes to Sleepy Hollow for answers. And those who've tried only leave with more questions."

"Or they don't leave at all," Rose mumbles from behind me.

Matilda's eyes flash an otherworldly red. "I suggest you two do the smart thing and follow suit."

With that, the vampire gets up and disappears deeper into the store after the witch and the demon.

Rose stares into her coffee cup as we sit curled up in our winter coats in the back corner of a 24-hour diner called The Sentinel. The early November winds seem to find their way through every crack and fissure of the poorly heated building.

The waitress, a tall Black woman with long braids that she's decorated with various silver charms and bells, smiles at me as she reaches our table, refilling my mug to the brim.

"Can I get you anything else, hon?" she asks with a smile that, unlike mine, doesn't seem at all rehearsed.

I shake my head. "I think we're good for now."

The waitress nods. "Holler if you need anything."

I do my best to offer a genuine smile then watch as she walks away. I find myself checking out her ass in the tight jeans she's wearing. Damnit, one interaction with a hot vampire and now I'm thirsty as hell for every woman I encounter. I feel no better than a man with the way I'm ogling them in public. I look at my sister, pulling my thoughts back to the present issue at hand.

"Rose," I prompt. "Say something."

"I was prepared for witches. Demons and vampires sounds like a lot for us to go up against."

I sigh. "We're not *going up against* anyone. This isn't an episode of *True Blood,* we're investigating missing persons cases in order to craft a narrative."

Rose rolls her eyes. "I'm familiar with our job, thank you. Still, an actual vampire? That's a lot. It's not like we're ghost hunters."

"Good thing Matilda isn't a ghost."

Rose aggressively sips her coffee. "So what?" She sets her mug back down. "We confront her with a stake and some garlic?"

Stake and garlic: cannot confirm or deny.

"I don't know if those things actually work." I pick up my own coffee and take a tentative sip.

"So you're an expert now?"

Now I'm the one who rolls my eyes. "Even if they did and we got her to confess to what she is on tape it's not like that would matter. No one's going to believe that. So why not at least try to get *something* out of her?"

"You know there are lots of people here and in other spooky places like Salem that claim to live a vampire lifestyle so if we did get her to make a full on vampiric confession on tape, it wouldn't be a totally tin foil hat take for a paranormal podcast."

"Do you think Arnold would go for that?" I ask.

Arnold, our producer, can't stand us and thinks our

entire show is a joke and makes it known quite often how pissed he is that he got assigned to some 'clueless newbies.'

"Who cares what Arnold wants," she huffs, knowing full well that we need to care what he wants if *we* want to keep our show on the network. "If we get enough hits on this episode then it won't matter." That's true enough. "Let's start with the obvious. Samantha Waverly Kos and her pet demon killed those men."

CHAPTER 2

I LIKE TO DO IT. I ENJOY IT.

MATILDA

My body was always rife with pain long before I died. Medicine was magic back then, therefore practically nonexistent if you weren't willing to seek out a proper midwife, or a fearsome witch. I was a dutiful Christian daughter who dared not disobey her parents so my aches and pains were viewed as penance and punishment that, if I were devout enough, could be properly prayed away. Nowadays there are long complicated words and fancy medicines sold in plastic bottles on the shelves of linoleum-floored stores with flickering fluorescent lights that boast to remedy ailments we didn't even know what to call back when I was alive.

Still, according to the first hand accounts I've seen on the rare occasions I use one of the social media apps on my phone, treatment for such issues is likely to not be done properly if the person in need is a woman.

Not that I can go to a doctor. I bleed black, my heart is silent in my chest, my pulse nonexistent. A dentist might have an aneurism if they were to figure out how old my teeth are. Back when the light was leaving my eyes and the blood was draining from my body and I was saying goodbye to the rejuvenating feeling of the sun on my skin one last time, I hoped that the pain would dissipate with my death. It was what I was promised. It was why I chose this eternity. What is a normal life riddled with agony for forever in physical bliss.

What a cruel joke.

I doubt my maker knew he was lying. I doubt he cared one way or the other, anything to convince me. He liked the power turning mortals gave him. He liked to drink from me even after he turned me, as he did with all the women who came before me. He drank so deep and long that it weakened me more than the sun. I put an end to it one day, buried his bones deep in the earth to rot with the worms.

Then I was alone in a big, terrible world with the same old aching body as before.

Lucky for me, blood is the best pain killer. The purer the blood—the less polluted it is by alcohol and drugs—the sweeter and stronger the effect. If I'm ever having a bad flare I can slink through the streets and find an unsuspecting late night soul to feast on and cure me—albeit briefly—of my ailments.

Tonight my body burns with fiery muscle pain and my stomach grumbles with unholy hunger. Most vampires my age are reserved with their hunting, skilled at controlling their hunger, but not me. Maybe it's the pain, maybe I've always been an insatiable being, maybe a life spent bowing to the whims of men has left me spending eternity delighting in ripping out the throats of any foolish enough to cross my path (not that I object to drinking women dry, their blood is often sweeter, but men are easier to kill).

I think about Octavia's attitude, her subtle supernatural ability, and her effervescent smile. She has unmoored me, it's a familiar feeling but not one I welcome. I picture her neck, the veins burning beautifully blue beneath her skin, the way her cheeks flushed, the hum of her blood. My stomach lurches with memories I never thought would matter.

Another muscle spasm stabs through me and I groan. My pain flare is too extreme to exert a wealth of physical energy. I can't settle for a simple kill tonight, I need some ambiance and comfort for my dinner, not a dank, dark alley.

With an exasperated sigh, I get dressed and head out into the night.

I'VE BARELY MADE it two steps out of my house before Sandy appears by my side. He's always doing that. Materializing out of a cloud of black sand and smoke, swirling in like a cyclone. How very Ozian of him. It's annoying and I'm sure it has been the cause of more than a few mortals' sneezing fits. I wonder how many bouts of allergies have really just been brought on by his age old habit of making a dramatic entrance.

Tonight he's chosen one of his less terrifying forms. Instead of swirling shadows and horrifying red eyes, he is all pale shining skin and spiky black hair. A long black coat hides him like a shroud, its color ebbs and flows, woven from the very shadows he commands.

"What do you want, Sandy?"

"Good evening to you too, Matilda. And you know I loathe when you call me that."

I smirk. "Why do you think I do it?"

Sandy grumbles but doesn't antagonize me. We walk on in silence until I reach the alley with the moving bricks that lead to The Underground.

"*Do* you want something?" I ask. "Or just stopping by to antagonize me?"

"I don't antagonize you, darling. You're my oldest and dearest friend."

"Exactly my point."

Sandy laughs, his coat swishing around him as we turn down the alley, his skin glinting in the moonlight as his laugh—silent to all but me—reverberates through the air.

"There's some newcomers in town. I heard they're asking questions."

"And who told you that?"

"Them. I heard their dreams. The one with brown hair has loud ones. Nightmares. Salty and sweaty."

I approach the bricks and tap them in the appropriate order, my bones rattling with more than pain. "Are you coming along?" I do not wish to speak of Octavia in any capacity. Not with him. Not with anyone.

Sandy quirks one corner of his glimmering mouth up in an almost smirk. "Not my scene, darling. Be careful."

"They're podcasters, not vampire slayers."

"You never know, they could be both."

I scoff as the bricks part to reveal a beautiful marble door that glimmers like starlight. "You're ridiculous. They're not going to be at The Back Room, they're not of our kind."

"Perhaps, but Arletta Harrington might be there."

At that I laugh. "What do I have to fear from that annoying little girl?"

"Word on the street is she's after Death."

Sandy dissolves into glittering dust, leaving me solitary before the door to the winding roads us paranormal folk walk late at night. I sigh at my friend's ambiguous warning and turn the knob. The roads of The Underground, as always, take me where I need to go and a few minutes later I emerge in The Back Room, a bar for people like me. The space is crowded tonight with all sorts of supernatural beings; pixies, fairies, selkies without their seal skin, swamp creatures, witches, werewolves, a couple of aufhockers, and of course vampires. The cursed Arletta is nowhere to be seen, but I do spy Samantha and Al in the corner. She's sitting on his lap, swishing a drink in her hand as he twirls a lock of her hair around his finger. The two are nauseating.

I make my way over.

"Hi, Matilda." Samantha beams at me like she didn't just see me at work a few hours ago.

"Hey, fangs." Al doffs an invisible cap to me.

If I could rip out his throat, I would. I have no idea what Samantha sees in him, but humans like her have always evaded my understanding, even when I was one of them.

"Al and I have to tell you something," Samantha continues. "I didn't get the chance to at work. It got so busy after the podcasters left."

I find myself clenching my jaw. The fact that Octavia's name seems to follow me like a shadow tonight makes me want to curse ancient gods and tear tendons from necks. I listen to those cheap paranormal and true crime podcasts for amusement. I don't need those sleazy, attention seeking types crowding my establishment and my life. And I especially don't need them poking around looking for the truth about what really happens here in the Hollow when the humans go to sleep and us monsters come out to play.

"Yes, you really did a good job of throwing them off the scent by praising the death of Ethan and Peyton." I eye Samantha's neck as I sit down across from her. I've often thought about drinking from her. I imagine her blood would be heady and rich, like the herbs she peddles. But drinking from my sole employee would be messy, especially now that she has a demon lover on a leash at all times. Al was annoying enough before being summoned, but now he's a downright menace.

Samantha rolls her eyes at my remark. I wave down Patrocles, the fae behind the bar, signaling that I want my usual.

"I didn't *praise* their death," Samantha insists.

"Right, babes," Al cuts in. "You just said you were glad they were dead. Not suspicious at all."

Samantha ignores his comment and sips her drink. "Well speaking of suspicious—Matilda, are you listening?"

Patrocles walks over with a silver tray balanced on his large palm, a goblet full of blood resting on top. I take it and slide him a twenty dollar bill.

"Evening, Matilda, always good to see you."

"You as well, Patrocles." I sip my blood. It's thick and sweet like honey, must've come from a fairy. Immediately as it washes through my system the spasming and stabbing sensations peppered across my back dull to a tolerable ache. After a few more sips the pain is merely a phantom in my bones, nothing more than the memory of agony. I think fleetingly of the cane the one podcaster was using. I wonder if she's always in pain too. I wonder if that pain has a name.

Patrocles nods at my companions. "Samantha, Al, always a pleasure."

Samantha smiles, Al salutes him. Once Patrocles has

retreated back behind the bar, I turn my attention to Samantha.

"Alright, I'm paying attention now, what is it?"

"That one podcaster, Octavia, the short one with brown hair—"

"Yes, I remember."

"She could see Al."

Samantha's words register with me as I'm taking another, rather large, gulp of my drink. I nearly choke on the liquid as it goes down. I quickly wipe stray blood droplets from around my lips and focus my burning eyes back on the goth by my side. "She could *what?*" Even as the words leave my lips I know the gravity of what Samantha's said. Of course Octavia is a seer. It all makes sense after all these years.

"She's a seer, Matilda. Which means she knows I'm a witch and she probably knows you're a vampire."

"And—" Al says. "That means she probably knows Arletta isn't actually dead."

I hate the demon most of the time, especially when he's right.

CHAPTER 3
DIABOLICAL FORCES ARE FORMIDABLE

OCTAVIA

Sometimes I think the gods hate me.

Sometimes I think I've been blessed with amazing luck.

Tonight proves to be the latter when I leave The Ichabod, the old timey inn we're staying in, to smoke and see a figure emerge in the alley across the street, seemingly out of the shadows. It's three a.m. The Witching Hour. The figure leans up against the wall and takes something out of their pocket. I see them strike a match and a tiny flame bursts into bloom. Even from across the street, in the dim glow of the cigarette, I can make out that the figure is Matilda. I watch her smoke for a few minutes, shoving my anxiety down my throat, building up my courage brick by brick until I'm a wall of determination.

I put out my own cigarette, open the audio recording app on my phone and press the red button before tucking it away in my jacket. I hurry across the street, my breath coming out like a dragon's as the bitter, nearly winter night, weighs down on me.

I approach her slowly and clear my throat."Smoking kills, you know."

The vampiress looks up at me and smiles, clearly smelling the smoke on my own clothes. "So does this town." She flicks some ash from her cigarette on the ground before placing the vice back between burgundy painted lips. The color of rich wine. The color of blood. "That's what you're here to prove, isn't it, Octavia?"

"Call me Via. And I'm not trying to prove that people died here. Everyone knows they did. I'm trying to gather credible evidence that the deaths of Peyton Kos and Ethan Steen were caused by supernatural forces."

Matilda drops her cigarette butt to the ground and stubs it out with the tip of her boot. "Supernatural forces like me?"

I swallow the lump in my throat, my tongue going dry. Matilda smiles at me, eyes like a siren's voice.

"Well," I clear my throat. "It was *your* party. I don't think you would be that messy at your own house."

"Is that so?" I nod. "So who do you think did it?"

"Samantha."

"And her demon pet?"

Based on the way Matilda is smirking, biting back obvious laughter, I must look gobsmacked. She's succeeding far too easily at making me feel like a fool.

"Al told us you can see him," Matilda says.

"His name is Al?"

She puts her hands in her pockets and stands up straight from the wall. "No, it's not." She smirks again.

I can't figure out why she's lurking in this alley in a mostly residential area. Does she live near here? She looks dolled up like she's been out on the town, but Sleepy Hollow isn't exactly a clubbing hot spot and the closest tavern is nowhere near here. I didn't even see her walking down the street before she appeared in this alley. I look to the side, but the alley leads to a dead end brick wall, no pub-laden street to dump her out on. *What* is she doing here?

"So did they do it?" I ask, fighting to quell my rising unease, my rioting internal doubts as I try to rationalize that what I think, what I remember, isn't true—*can't* be true. "The two of them."

She takes a step closer to me, her tall frame looming over mine, the chunky heels of her boots aiding to the intimidation effect. She smells like tobacco, wine, and poppies. The scent is overwhelming, wafting over me like an enchanting elixir. I don't know if it's her obviously raw sex appeal or her vampire persuasive powers that are affecting me so heavily, but either way this situation seems increasingly dangerous.

Matilda gives me a decorous smile, head tilted down just right to meet my gaze. "I have a question of my own, Via. Why are you pretending you don't recognize me?"

Her words are an anvil. I'm crushed, smashed flat on the pavement alongside her discarded cigarette. My cheeks flush and sweat pools in my armpits, all the while the vampire keeps smiling.

The memory I've been trying to suppress since I first saw her in the bookshop crashes over me now, a tidal wave I can't escape: a night when I was no more than sixteen years old. I awoke from a nightmare to a piercing pain in my chest like two thin needles puncturing me just above my heart. I sat up gasping, to see a beautiful woman crouched at the foot of my bed. She was clad in a white nightgown like something out of a German Expressionist film, her dark hair falling across her shoulders in cascading waves of ebony with a gentle curl. Her skin practically glowed in the moonlight. She was perfection incarnate and her mouth was covered in my blood. I often thought I dreamed her. But then I would brush my fingers across the faint scar over my heart and know the truth.

I do so now. My bulky coat gets in the way, but I still carry out the motion of pressing my fingers over my heart, knowing the tiny scar, nearly invisible all these years later, resides there. A permanent reminder of her teeth in my flesh. The maiden monster who crawled into my bed when I was so young I barely understood my own supernatural abilities.

"Did you think I was a dream?" Matilda stalks closer.

I drop my hand. "Never."

She smiles viciously, pushing me back against the wall with one hand on my shoulder mere inches from my scarred heart.

"You came here to hunt monsters, dearie? Well done, you found one. But there's a slight problem with your plan." She leans in close, her dark lips feather light against my ear, her breath hot in the chilly November night. "You'll never be able to catch us."

She nips roughly at my ear, I cry out in surprise more so than in pain. Matilda laughs maniacally then vanishes into the night.

CHAPTER 4

COME FREELY,
GO SAFELY.

MATILDA

"That podcaster is really pissing me off." I light a cigarette and inhale. Samantha groans and opens the tiny window in my office at the back of The Raven's Quill.

"Which one?" Al asks.

"The short one." I exhale out the window. Samantha lights some sage she has in her pocket because *of course* the herbalist keeps sage on her person.

"Did you talk to her like you said you would?" Samantha asks, waving the sage around, filling the tiny room up with *more* smoke. Al pretends to cough dramatically, Samantha just smiles like he's the cutest puppy in the world. It's disgusting.

"Yes. But she seems too stupid to back down."

"Speaking of backing down," Al says. "Heard from Patrocles that they're running low on real blood at The Back Room. Sounds like they're only gonna be selling the synthetic stuff for a while."

"What?" I cough a bit on prematurely exhaled smoke and blink through tears against the stupid sage smoke wafting in my eyes. "Why?"

Synthetic blood is some mysterious drink crafted in an underground lab somewhere in Scotland by a mad scientist that puts Frankenstein to shame. It tastes like cough syrup and hardly sates even the most ancient vampire's thirst. But when you're stuck somewhere with a dwindling population or overly nosy neighbors and you can't afford the pricey blood cocktails here at The Backroom, it's the only way to stay alive. But it's no way to *live*.

"Ahhhh." Al floats up to sit on top of my desk where I have my feet propped up. With a flourish he knocks them out of his way. Gods, I hate him. "Probably because the fae folk who run the joint don't wanna take down humans and the fae folk who *don't* run the joint are sick of giving their blood up to be dinner. Besides—" he conjures a pre-lit cigarette, Samantha groans at the newest addition of smoke. "—the rest of the paranormal community doesn't exactly love vamps."

I flick my cigarette at him and smile in satisfaction as it singes his shirt.

"Matilda!" Samantha shrieks, waving her hand to extinguish it. "Are you trying to set the shop on fire?"

I ignore her and head out to the front of the store. As soon as I emerge from the beaded curtains we recently hung in the doorway between my office and the back of the cash register, I immediately regret my decision.

Octavia and Rose stand in front of me, podcast equipment in hand.

"What do you want?" I snap. I'm already in a bad mood today from aching muscles and burning joints and now I'm going to have to get my dinner myself—raw. I suppose I'll go lurk around one of the human bars.

Al killing Ethan and Peyton was a real pain. They were so easy to allure and drink from. I left their sorry, drunk asses passed out in the alley behind their favorite pub more times than I can count. I was planning to drink from Peyton the night of my Halloween party before Samantha sicked her little beast on him. Now I have to start fresh, scope out new victims. Perhaps I'll finally resort back to stalking children. They're the easiest to catch unaware and leave dazed and wondering if it was all a dream.

All children except Octavia Majestic.

The irksome little seer continues to be impervious to my powers. I recognized her the second she stepped into my store yesterday, but thought surely it couldn't be her. It had to have been at least a decade since I crawled into the bed of that lonely, little girl who called out for a friend. Octavia—*Via*—while somewhat of a nervous creature, possessed none of the timid nature of that girl in the bed. But then the way her whole body quivered against me when I dared call her out on that night proved all of my suspicions true.

Via and I have met before. Once upon a dream ago.

Today she has her winter coat unbuttoned and the t-shirt she's wearing beneath has the collar cut off in a raggedy, crooked line, swooping down low enough over her chest so that I can make out the faint scar above her heart that my mouth left on her ages ago. I can't help but smile at the sight. If she's hoping I'm going to feel some sort of sympathy for her, she's terribly mistaken.

"We're here to ask you for an interview," her sister, Rose says.

I glance at her, with her pale skin and red hair, she looks

nothing like her sister. I wonder if they're adopted. Via has brown skin and dark hair, her features similar to Samantha's. Maybe she's Mexican like her (this is where Samantha would insist that I not forget that she's half Slovenian to which I would reply: *Well, I'm 100% Slovenian, dearie* and then she would huff and remind me that it's *not a competition*).

"Did my employee and myself not make it clear yesterday that we have no desire to speak with you two?"

Via rolls her eyes with a dramatic sigh, it's a small act of defiance but is still certainly a step up from the obvious panicking she was exhibiting yesterday. "We're not asking you to come on the pod and declare that you're a vampire or that your friend killed her brother and—"

"I didn't kill him." Samantha storms out from behind the jingling bead curtain, Al, as always, lurking behind her.

"Right." Via narrows her eyes. "He did." She points to Al who just starts laughing.

"Well," he straightens his tie. "I had always hoped my big break would be on the silver screen, but I suppose a rinky dink podcast will do."

"It's not rinky dink!" Via says.

Al laughs louder.

Rose just looks confused. It seems Via's sister does not possess any otherworldly powers.

"You can't be interviewed," Samantha reminds Al. "Don't be dumb." She hoists herself onto the counter and swings her legs over to dangle off the other side so she's facing the sisters. "You ladies better have a more convincing pitch or I'm going to put a hex on you every time you try to enter this store."

I stifle a laugh. Samantha doesn't have a single hexing

bone in her body. She would need to enlist her beloved Arletta to achieve any kind of negative magic.

"We do," Via insists. "Our episode is focussing primarily on the lore of dullahans. Do an interview with us and give us a story about how you saw the Headless Horseman that night." She looks past Samantha, directly at me. "At *your* party."

"You know—" I lean one hand on the counter to take some of the weight off my aching knees as I walk around the side, out to the main floor, standing practically toe-to-toe with my former prey. "Most people think the Headless Horseman is just a myth."

Via smirks. "Yeah. Most people say the same thing about vampires too."

SPOOK STREET PODCAST EP. 19: DULLAHANS &
WHERE THEY LURK (transcript excerpt)

OCTAVIA:
Do you know about the Legend of Arletta
Harrington?

ROSE:
No, is it similar to The Legend of Sleepy
Hollow?

OCTAVIA:
It's adjacent to that story.

ROSE:
Do tell.

OCTAVIA:
So several years ago in Sleepy Hollow there
lived a witch.

ROSE:
Naturally.

OCTAVIA:
And the locals hated her.

ROSE:
Tale as old as time.

OCTAVIA:
One Halloween night she goes out for a walk
and is never seen again. A huge

investigation opens up, there are several suspects in her disappearance, including Ethan Steen and Payton Kos, the men who died at Matilda Sherridan's Halloween party a month ago. So the question remains, did Arletta come back from the dead to off her killers? *Were* they the killers? Or did Arletta never die?

ROSE:
If she never died, where did she go?

OCTAVIA:
That's what we're headed to Sleepy Hollow to find out.

CHAPTER 5

GHOSTS ARE REAL. THIS MUCH I KNOW.

OCTAVIA

We make quite the odd assembly walking through the streets of Sleepy Hollow back to Matilda's house. Rose and I had to wait until the bookshop was closed for the day before Matilda and Samantha would agree to meet with us. So we spent the rest of the afternoon and early evening lurking around town trying to find anything or anyone helpful to speak with. We eventually made our way to the cemetery and the grave of the infamous Arletta Harrington. There was nothing about it that stood out and screamed SHE'S ACTUALLY STILL ALIVE AND THIS IS ALL AN ELABORATE FARCE TO COVER UP THE FACT THAT SHE RAN AWAY WITH A MYTHICAL BEING, which was disappointing and makes our job more difficult. So now we follow a vampire, a witch, and a demon down the road (it sounds like the start of a bad joke).

It's a short walk to Matilda's house, but I can tell Rose is struggling. I once again tried and failed to convince her to take her walker. I know she hates it and it's harder to maneuver in tight spaces than her cane, but all this walking is clearly getting the best of her. I make a mental note to pick up some ice on the way back to the inn.

Matilda's home is almost comically vampiric; a looming, gothic house that looks like it fell out of the pages of a work by Mary Shelley.

Matilda leads us through the iron gate and up the steps where she takes a Secret Garden-eque key out of her bag and unlocks the door—because apparently the gods decided this needed to be the most cliche endeavor ever experienced by two paranormal podcasters. The inside of Matilda's home proves to be just as ridiculously gothic as the outside. There's art on the walls that I'm sure Rose can identify (I failed my art history class in college but Rose aced it, she dragged me to the immersive Monet exhibit three times last summer), fancy rugs running down the seemingly endless hallways and a grand staircase at the end of the honest to god foyer we're crowded in. I tilt my head back and see that a chandelier hangs above us, massive and glittering. I glance over at Rose who shoots me a look that conveys she's equally astonished by this not so humble abode.

"This way," Matilda says.

We follow her into a room that I can only describe as a parlor. Samantha takes a seat on one of the sofas, clearly comfortable in this space that must be familiar to her. Al glides over and sits beside her, taking her hand in his. The two seem to always need physical contact with one another, as if it were second nature to them. Matilda sits in a wingback chair at the far end of the room, her posture is regal as she gazes over the space. She waves a hand to the free sofa on the opposite side of her chair, eyes burning into me. Rose lightly nudges my foot with her cane and we go sit down.

"Get out the podcast stuff." Matilda waves her hand in the air like she's already bored with us (she probably is).

"Podcast equipment," Samantha corrects her. Matilda rolls her eyes.

Al leans back on the couch, grinning in a taunting way. "I can't wait to see this."

Rose and I ignore him (it's easier for her to do so since she can't see or hear him) and begin setting up our equipment. Once we've properly hooked up all of our mics and Rose has the recording software open on her laptop, we begin.

"Today my sister Rose and I are joined by two very special guests: Sleepy Hollow locals Samantha Waverly Kos and Matilda Sheridan. You two work at The Raven's Quill, correct?"

Samantha is quick to lift the mic near her mouth, her eyes bright. She might actually be eager to do this. "Matilda owns the bookshop, I just work there."

Matilda eyes Samantha who gives her a nod of encouragement. Matilda sighs and relents to lifting her own mic. "My star employee is being modest. She does more than *just* work in my bookstore. She's also the town's herbalist."

"So, Samantha, you're a witch?" Rose asks. My sister is never one to beat around the bush.

I'm fully prepared for Samantha to snap at her but she just offers a demure smile in return. "If you say so."

Rose glances at me but I can't seem to tear my gaze away from Matilda, who's returning my stare in kind. The corner of her mouth is quirked up in an almost smirk. She's studying me, trying to draw me out, but I'm not sure what it is that she's looking for. She's already gotten me to admit that I remember her from my childhood and she knows that I'm a seer. I don't have any more secrets and I've been candid about why Rose and I are here in town, we don't have any hidden agenda. Maybe she's trying to figure out if I'm gay.

I need to get it together. I don't even know if *she's* gay.

People say all vampires are queer and yes, vampire media is steeped in a history of queer and sexual repression, but that doesn't mean that this particular vampire is gay.

But I *really* hope she is.

I'm ready to have a full Bella Swan moment, however knowingly stupid, dangerous, and unprofessional that is.

"And you both knew Ethan Steen and Peyton Kos?" Rose asks them, pulling me from my sapphic thought spiral.

"Yes." Matilda smiles at me, tight-lipped, eyes taunting. "We knew them."

Al laughs. Samantha slaps his leg in chastisement. He grabs the hand that did the slapping, brings it to his mouth and kisses it. She blushes. The entire display is gross. I still don't understand why this herbalist witch has a demon pet. I glance at my sister who is obviously confused why Samantha just smacked the air. I bump my shoulder against Rose's and mouth 'the demon.' Her eyes widen and she gives a subtle nod.

Samantha turns her attention back to us. "It's no secret to anyone that Peyton was my half-brother. I didn't know Ethan as well as Matilda."

"Were you and Ethan friends?" I ask Matilda.

"Of a sort."

She's so hot when she's being a bitch.

"Ethan was Arletta's ex," Samantha says, her smile faltering. "He and Peyton were friends."

"But you weren't close with your brother?" Rose presses.

Samantha's eyes narrow at us. I'm trying to figure out why on earth she's glad her brother is dead. From what little I was able to find out about her from her minimal online presence, he was her only living family.

"No," Samantha says. "We weren't. My *half* brother was a terrible person. He did terrible things. So did Ethan."

"What did Ethan do?" I ask, then before Samantha can get pissed at me (again), I clarify: "I know you mentioned something yesterday, but if you could restate what you... um...told us just so we have your account for the episode." I gesture to the mics in front of us like an awkward idiot who feels the need to remind everyone that we're recording a podcast.

I notice Al's squeezing Samantha's knee, like he's trying to stop a volcano from erupting.

"Ethan was cruel to Arletta." Samantha's voice is hollow and cold, no sign of the vitriol she spewed at us when the topic of Ethan came up at the bookstore yesterday. "Violent. Abusive. And when Arletta found the courage to leave him, he told the whole town lies about her. Convinced them that she practiced dark magic. He turned everyone against her."

"Even you two?" I ask.

Matilda scoffs.

Samantha looks furious. "I wasn't close with Arletta then. She was always a bit of a recluse, but I never believed Ethan's lies. I never held any respect for people who respected Peyton."

"What about you?" I look at Matilda.

Matilda shrugs. "Samantha has a kinder heart than me. Ethan and Peyton were my acquaintances, people I invited to parties or said hello to at the bar. I didn't know about their dark secrets and I didn't care to. Samantha and I weren't friends yet, she was just my employee so it never occurred to me to inquire about why she was no contact with her—" Matilda glances at Samantha briefly. "—*half* brother. Now I know better."

"Did you believe Ethan about Arletta?" Rose asks.

Matilda scoffs again. "I don't care about Arletta Harrington. I never have. I know Samantha was her best friend. But not me. I found her irksome and annoyingly shrewd."

"That doesn't answer the question," I snap.

Matilda smirks. "Yes. I believed him. If you had met Arletta you would have seen why it was so easy to believe. She was sharp and vicious. She claimed to just be a divination witch but there was always something dark about her."

"Matilda," Samantha cuts in. "That's enough." Samantha looks at me. "Arletta is—*was* a diviner."

I glance at Rose, the look in my sister's eyes tells me she also caught Samantha's slip up. My theory strengthens.

"But *was* she a witch?" Rose presses Samantha. "Like you?"

"I'm an herbalist. Arletta was a diviner."

"But you two are *both* witches, right?" My sister is hammering down hard.

Samantha plasters her fake smile back on. "Herbalists and diviners have been around for centuries. If people want to use the word 'witch' when discussing such things, then who am I to stop them?"

An uneasy silence settles over the room. Matilda and

Samantha are good at dodging the truth. We all know they're clearly hiding the real story about what really happened to Arletta Harrington.

"What happened on Halloween when Arletta went missing?" I ask, haughtily.

Samantha shrugs. "I wasn't there."

"What about you?" I look at Matilda.

"I was having my annual Halloween party. I didn't even know she was missing until the next day when Samantha came into work."

"Do you think Arletta is dead?" I ask.

The uneasy energy returns with snapping jaws this time, tearing away at the tension and leaving a ragged, bloody silence in its wake. Samantha leans forward, elbows on her knees, brows furrowed in a blatant glare.

"Arletta Harrington was declared dead years ago after she had been missing for several months with no leads in her disappearance. She has a tombstone in the cemetery. I visit it often. I can show it to you if you'd like."

"We've seen it," Rose says.

"Then there you have it," Al says, deciding to unofficially join the interview.

"Well," I continue, unable to back down now. "There are those who believe Arletta chose to go missing. Some people even believe she ran away with the Headless Horseman and now rides with him every Samhain as his ghostly companion."

Samantha is the one to smirk this time. "That's quite the tall tale."

"Do you believe it?" I stare into Samantha's brown eyes, searching for the truth behind the web of lies she's weaving.

"I believe that my best friend passed over to the world

of the dead and never came back. If people who never knew her want to believe that a magical, mythical being took her away, they're welcome to."

I glance at my sister, she offers me a small shrug. It's clear she doesn't know what else to ask.

But I do.

"Do either of you believe in the Headless Horseman?"

They both laugh.

"This *is* Sleepy Hollow," I insist. "Don't most people here believe in his existence?"

"Most people are fools." Matilda waves off my question like an annoying bug.

"Do *you two* believe in him?" Samantha taunts.

"We believe in finding the truth," my sister says.

Al laughs again before speaking boldly, knowing that his demonic voice won't be picked up by our low budget mics, let alone even heard by Rose. "You ladies want the truth? You think Arletta and her headless lover killed Ethan and Peyton?"

I bite my tongue, Rose's jaw clenches. I can see in Samantha's eyes that she doesn't believe we believe that.

"I hate to break it to you, ladies, but you're way off the mark, Al laughs.

"I'm sorry," Rose snaps. "Is the ghost talking? Is that why you three are staring at the empty spot on the couch?"

"Demon," Al clarifies.

"Demon," I repeat for Rose. "Yeah. The demon is talking."

"Well, what did he say?"

Matilda sighs dramatically, my sister's inability to commune with spirits is apparently a very dull affair to her.

"He *said*," Samantha cuts in. "That you two are way off

the mark with your *theories* around who killed Ethan and Peyton."

"And how does he know that?" Rose's voice is tinged with annoyance.

This interview has really gone off the rails.

"Because," Al grins, his eyes lanced on mine. "I killed them."

CHAPTER 6

HELLOS, GOODBYES, A THOUSAND MIDNIGHTS LOST IN SLEEPLESS LULLABIES

OCTAVIA

I can't sleep.

I sit on the cold steps of the inn and chain smoke as I try to figure out what to do. Theoretically we have enough to piece together a decent episode. Arnold won't be too disappointed (hopefully). It's not like this is a true crime case we can crack with a demon's confession. The first thing we did when we got back to our room at The Ichabod was play our recording back and as I suspected, Al's voice didn't pick up. Just static.

We can go home, turn in the content we've gathered and move onto the next episode. But something tugs at me to stay. Just a bit longer. I could say it's because I personally want to know the truth about what happened to Arletta, but I'd be lying.

I want to see Matilda again.

I watch the alley across the street through my plumes of exhaled smoke and hope I see her arrive. Just when I'm about to give up and return to our room and crawl into the

King sized bed I'm sharing with Rose, I see Matilda walking down the street, her long coat billowing behind her like a cape. There's a man with her. He's tall, lanky, and his skin has a slight blue hue to it, his hair is ink black and hangs down to his shoulders. It's blatantly clear to me that he's not human. But I can't quite pinpoint what kind of being he is. All I know is that whatever he is, he's the only one of his kind.

Matilda stops at the entrance to the alleyway and turns to face me. I drop my cigarette to the ground and stamp it out. I unnecessarily adjust my glasses. Matilda smirks. The strange man with her looks a bit perplexed.

"Well, come on then," she calls out to me.

With absolutely no chill or aloofness, I race across the street so fast I nearly trip. Matilda laughs as I come to stand before her and her mystery companion.

"Hi," I gasp, my breath turning to smoke of its own in the chilly air.

Matilda smiles, this time it's not completely taunting. "Hello, Via."

I smile at the sound of my nickname on her tongue. I want her tongue in my mouth. Badly.

I look at the man and hold out my hand (hoping it's not obvious how badly it's shaking). "Hi, I'm Octavia Majestic. But you can just call me Via."

I always worry that I sound painfully rehearsed whenever I give this spiel, but Rose has assured me I sound totally natural whenever I do it. *It's a good opener,* she always assures me. I tend to watch in awe whenever Rose introduces herself like it's the easiest thing in the world, making friends wherever we go. Ma always said Rose collected friends with a butterfly net. If that's true then I catch friends with a glue trap. Awkward, sticky, unsettling.

The strange being smiles, his eyes like glowing black orbs, nary a pupil in sight. His skin seems like it's made of starlight and a sort of glittering dust seems to float around him. I realize who he is before he speaks his name.

"Hello, Via." He shakes my hand, his skin is ice cold and leaves a trace of glittery dust on my palm. "My name is—"

"This is my good friend, Sandy," Matilda cuts in, smirking as she pats him roughly on the arm.

The man, whose name I'm positive isn't actually 'Sandy', sighs. I'm sure if he had normal eyes they would be rolling right about now. "My name is not Sandy, it is Ole Lukøie."

I exhale softly in awe. "You're The Sandman."

He nods. "Indeed I am. You can call me Luk."

"Or Sandy," Matilda says.

Luk sighs again and shoves Matilda who just laughs. "Do not call me Sandy, Via, I beg of you. I can barely tolerate hearing it from her all of the time."

I glance at Matilda. "You're friends with The Sandman?"

Matilda shrugs. "When you've been dead for as long as I have, you meet a lot of *interesting* people."

"How long *have* you been around?"

Matilda doesn't answer me. She takes my hand in hers, glitter passing from palm to palm, and leads me down the alley to the spot in the brick wall where I saw her standing last night. Luk glides along behind us, his feet seeming to never fully touch the ground.

Matilda looks back at Luk. "Are you coming with us?"

"Where are we going?" I ask.

She ignores me.

Luk smiles. His inky eyes make it an unsettling sight. "You know I don't go there, darling. But as always, thank you for the invite. I'll bid you goodnight." He turns and nods to me. "Goodnight, Seer Via. Be careful with this one."

Luk turns into glittering dust—or rather glittering *sand* —before our eyes. I glance at Matilda, she smirks and turns to face the wall. "Ready, dearie?"

"For what?"

She laughs again. I want to get drunk off the sound.

She taps the bricks in a specific pattern and then a door appears, nestled into the wall. It's a wide, wooden door with a surface that looks like it's made out of the night sky itself. My mouth falls open in surprise. All the years I've spent observing the supernatural, I've never gotten to truly be a part of this hidden underworld of existence. It was something that was always just out of reach to me.

The door opens up to a stone tunnel dimly lit by old fashioned street lanterns. Various other doors line the space every few feet and it bends off into different paths further down. I glance briefly at Matilda but she doesn't look back as she presses on forward, dragging me behind her. As soon as I've stepped over the threshold, the door closes behind us. For a split second I'm worried it's going to dissolve entirely and that Matilda has actually led me to my death, but thankfully the door remains very much present.

We walk a ways further into the tunnel, taking a few turns until we reach a door that's entirely black, such a deep inky shade that it almost shines. Instead of a door knob there's a large brass handle. Matilda pushes it open with one hand, the other still clasped in mine. Inside I had expected some fantasy dark academia space, but instead I'm surprised to see a very modern bar with neon lights and a dance floor full of scantily clad people that I can tell right away are all of the paranormal variety.

There's different types of the fae, werewolves,

vampires, witches, even a few ghosts. There are women with sleek skin that I can tell are selkie, some even wear their seal skins as garments; a slim skirt here, a flowing coat there. I can make out gaggles of pixies flitting around the dance floor, and a dragon-looking beast milling about the bar. It's a sensory overload of paranormal energy. There's so many witches letting their magic scent waft about them, uninhibited, it's like walking into an incense shop at the Renaissance Festival. I have to actively breathe through my mouth to make sure I don't get a headache. All of that coupled with the normal sensory issues loud bars give me and I think I might just pass out, but then Matilda squeezes my hand, almost comfortingly and it grounds me in this moment. I can breathe, my heart can beat at a normal pace, and I don't feel like I'm going to vomit or drop dead.

Matilda begins guiding me across the space to a cushioned set of seats along the back wall. As we get closer I fiddle with my glasses again, annoyingly surprised to see that Samantha and Al are tucked away in the corner, Samantha perched on Al's lap.

"What's their deal?" I ask Matilda as we approach.

Matilda looks down at me. "What do you mean?"

"Why does she have a demon for a pet?"

Matilda laughs and squeezes my hand again. She doesn't answer my question (a favorite pastime of hers, I'm learning). We make our way to the bench, the witch and demon look up as we approach, the heavy scent of brimstone lingers in the air.

"What's she doing here?" Samantha says, her voice like vinegar.

"She's a seer." Matilda states the obvious before she sits down next Samantha. When I don't follow suit she tugs me down beside her. Our thighs brush and my heart nearly explodes.

"Just because she can see us doesn't mean she's one of us." Samantha glares at me. "We did your podcast interview, why are you still hanging around?"

"Babes, are you arguing for paranormal species segregation?" Al chuckles.

"Really, Samantha," Matilda says. "I get enough of that as a vampire. I don't need you treating my new friend that way."

"She's not your friend," Samantha grumbles.

"Why don't other paranormal people like vampires?" I ask.

"Because, little lady," Al says. "Vampires aren't born vampires. The rest of us are born just the way we are."

"*You* were not born," Matilda says. She waves down the bartender, a beautiful fae man with dark skin, bright green eyes, and hair as long as a waterfall. When he sees Matilda's hand, he nods and starts to head our way.

"Same difference," Al says.

"So you guys hate vampires because they chose to be vampires?" I ask.

Samantha rolls her eyes, she clearly thinks I'm an idiot.

"Most vampires don't choose to be vampires. And *I* don't hate vampires, most paranormal people don't. It's an outdated mindset from the Burning Times. Matilda's being dramatic."

Matilda winks at me.

The fae man towers over us, smiling with unnaturally pearly white teeth that have inhumanely sharp edges.

"Matilda, who's your friend?" he asks.

"Patrocles, this is Octavia."

"Just Via," I tell him.

"Charmed." He smiles those ferocious teeth at me. "Can I get you a drink, Via?"

"Sure. Just a glass of cabernet if you have it."

He laughs like I've said the funniest thing (maybe I have, but I don't know what kind of drinks they sell in a bar like this).

"Can I have my usual?" Matilda asks.

I notice an uneasy tone to her voice, for the first time since meeting her she seems unsure.

"Sorry, love, didn't you hear? We've only got synthetic right now."

Matilda sighs. "I heard, I was just hoping it wasn't true."

"Sadly it is. Can I get you a glass of the stuff?"

Matilda shakes her head. "You know I loathe the stuff. I'll drink later." She nods towards me. "Put her drink on my tab."

"Sure thing." Patrocles smiles before walking back to the bar.

I glance at Matilda as she rests her hand casually on my thigh. "Thank you," I say.

"Don't mention it, dearie."

"They only have synthetic blood?" I ask.

"Wow, nothing gets past you," Al says.

Samantha laughs.

Matilda rakes her nails up my leg. I have jeans on but even with the thick fabric between our skin, my body is still set aflame from her touch.

"It's a shortage," she says breezily. "It will pass." She looks at Samantha. "Is she here yet?"

Samantha shakes her head, then takes her phone out from where she's tucked it down the front of her dress. The placement makes sense, her funeral attire doesn't seem to lend itself to pockets. She unlocks her phone and taps the screen a few times before looking back up at Matilda. "She's on her way. She's leaving The Archive now."

"I swear that woman practically lives there," Al says.

I want to ask what The Archive is and who they're talking about, but based on the limited time I've spent among these people I'm fairly confident they won't give me a straight answer, or *any* answer at all.

"So we have time." Matilda stands up, dramatically takes off her winter coat revealing the long, flowing Stevie Nicks type dress she has on beneath, and holds a hand out to me. "Care to dance, dearie?"

Entranced by the vampiric femme fatale I immediately get to my feet, shake off my far less glamorous winter coat, and take Matilda's hand. She guides me to the dance floor, a space cluttered with various paranormal creatures that dazzle and sparkle. Samantha's distaste for my presence rattles around in my mind. Do I count as supernatural because I can see what other humans can't? Matilda might think so even if Samantha doesn't. Al certainly doesn't seem to care and if Patrocles could tell I'm nothing special he certainly didn't show it. I wonder if whoever's coming from the place called The Archive will see me as supernatural or not.

We reach the center of the dance floor. Matilda puts her hands on my hips, pulls me in close, and suddenly all of my previous doubts and worries wash away. We move with the music, some techno remix of a David Bowie song. The lights are dim enough that Matilda's shrouded in an allusive darkness, but not so dim that I can't make out the vibrancy of her eyes. She smells like poppies and cigarette smoke again. Rose would be disgusted by the tobacco scent, but I adore it. I wonder if she'd taste like smoke if I were to kiss her.

"Is being a seer why I can't enthrall you like other humans?" Matilda asks, pulling me from my daze.

I nod. "Yeah. I think so. Can you enthrall other humans that have magic? Like Samantha?"

Matilda smirks. "Do you think you're magic, dearie?"

"Oh." So she doesn't think being a seer is anything worthy of the paranormal moniker. "I don't know. I just meant—"

She tugs playfully on a lock of my hair. "I jest. Being a seer is as magic as anything else. No, I can't enthrall Samantha. I can't enthrall any witches, their magic creates a wall between my power and theirs. I suppose the reason it doesn't work on you is because you can see through it. Can you tell when I'm trying to?"

I wrap my arms around her neck as the music shifts to a slower song. "I think so. Go ahead and try."

"I have been."

"Oh, what have you been trying to get me to do?"

Matilda's eyes flash red for just a second. The air between us ripples. Time flickers in and out of motion.

And then...

Matilda leans down and kisses me. The world around me explodes. Every other kiss before this one has been nothing but emptiness, this is what kissing should always be like. She *does* taste like smoke, peppermint, and a slight coppery tang. I push away the alarm bells about what that final flavor might be from and lose myself in her kiss. She licks the seam of my mouth, demanding entrance and I happily obey her. She digs her nails into my back, pulling me closer, getting me drunk off her taste. She digs her teeth into my bottom lip, not hard enough to break the skin, but enough to remind me fully of what she is.

I lurch away. She smirks at me, her red lipstick smeared slightly from the collision of our mouths. I inhale deeply, forcing myself to stop being so easily sucked in by her beauty and energy. She's dangerous. She's a predator. And from the way she talked about Arletta during the podcast interview, she seems like she's kind of a bitch. No, not seems like. She is. But gods damn do I want her to do terrible things to me.

"What's wrong, dearie?" She moves in close to me. "You didn't mind before."

I shove her back and she just laughs. "I was sixteen." My voice barely carries above the music. A few other people on the dance floor have glanced our way, but most of them are too busy enjoying their own evenings to care about whatever drama is stirring up between me and Matilda.

"Did you think you would never see me again?" she asks.

At that I scoff. Her arrogance is sickening. "Did you think I *wanted* to?"

"Seemed like it just now."

I turn and storm away from her, anger swelling up inside me. Anger at Matilda for creeping back into my life to take advantage of me like she did back then. Anger at myself for so easily becoming her prey once more. Anxiety, my old friend and constant companion, creeps back into me, wrapping itself around my bones, burrowing deep in my flesh. I try to do box breathing to prevent a full on panic attack. I make a beeline for the exit, refusing to look back. I reach the door and am about to push it open, not caring that I don't know the way back to the alley, when a woman with long dark hair, dressed so witchy that she looks like a walking stereotype, comes bursting through, a stack of books tucked under her arm. We collide and her books go falling to the floor. I curse softly, immediately ducking down to help her pick them up.

"Sorry," I mumble. "I was in a rush."

The woman takes the books from me and smiles. "No problem. Have a good night."

She passes me by, gliding like an ethereal being, her long black dress and cape flowing behind her, the pointy hat on top of her head remaining perfectly in place with each stride she takes. The scent of pumpkin mixed with a crackling fire lingers in the air. I watch the witch make her way across the bar and sit down next to Samantha and Al.

My world explodes a second time.

I just bumped into Arletta Harrington and she is very much alive.

CHAPTER 7

BUT DREAMS COME THROUGH STONE WALLS, LIGHT UP DARK ROOMS

MATILDA

"Who's coat is this?" Arletta picks up Via's winter coat as she sits down.

I scan across the room and see Via standing by the door, eyes glued to Arletta. I sigh. No surprise that the investigative podcaster knows what Arletta looks like. The diviner doesn't do her attempted ambiguity any favors by dressing like she's wearing a Halloween costume year round. Her tacky fashion sense never ceases to annoy me.

"Matilda's girlfriend's," Samantha says.

Arletta aggressively shoves me further down the cushioned seat so she can sit next to Samantha. I glare at her but she ignores me.

"You have a new girlfriend?" she asks.

I purse my lips and say nothing, watching as Via makes a beeline across the bar back over to us.

"Have you heard about the paranormal podcasters in town?" Al asks Arletta.

Arletta shoots him a sour look. She finds him as annoying as I find her. Sometimes I almost feel sorry for Samantha, being stuck in the middle of this. But she chose to be friends with Arletta and she chose to fuck a demon, I can't help it if I'm always irked by their presence. Perhaps my employee should find less vexing companions.

"Why would I have heard about that?" Arletta asks.

"Excuse me." Via says.

She doesn't look at me, she only has eyes for Arletta.

"Oh, here we go," Samantha grumbles.

I take Via's coat from Arletta's grip and stand up. I drape it over Via's shoulders but she still won't look at me.

"Are you Matilda's new girlfriend?" Arletta asks her.

That gets Via to decide to grace me with a look. "You have a girlfriend?"

"No." I snake an arm around her waist and pull her to my side.

Arletta scoffs.

"Are you Arletta Harrington?" Via just won't quit.

Arletta hesitates. She looks at Samantha and Al for some kind of confirmation as to who Via is. Plenty of people in here know Arletta, but none of them have ever asked her in such an awestruck way. Arletta shifts a bit closer to Samantha, her friend grabs her hand. They're ridiculous, you'd think they were hiding from being hanged at a witch trial. Nothing about Via is intimidating in the slightest. She's barely five feet tall and dressed like she stepped out of a hiker's catalog.

"That's one of the podcasters," Samantha says conspiratorially, like Via's presence in town is some secretive mission of espionage.

Via glances at me and then Samantha, but once again her eyes return to Arletta, glowing like she's gazing upon a movie star or a messiah.

"Yeah," Arletta says. "I'm her."

Via moves away from me and holds out her hand. "I'm Octavia Majestic."

Her voice pitches up, betraying her anxiety. It might not be noticeable to others, but after hearing her prattle on for a few days now I'm well-versed in what her at ease voice sounds like.

Arletta hesitantly shakes Via's hand. As soon as their palms touch Arletta's eyes widen and sparkle. She rips her hand away from Via's with a gasp. "You're a seer."

"You got that from a handshake?" Al asks, stretching his arms out across the back of the seat to wrap one across Samantha's shoulders. Via seems to be somewhat physically repulsed by the demon's show of physical affection. I can't say that I blame her.

"Arletta's powerful," Samantha says.

"Astounding." My voice is acidic. I reach for Via's hand, pulling her back to my side.

"If you're in town to uncover the secret of my death, I hate to disappoint you." Arletta drops Via's gaze and gets to work flipping through the pages of one of the many tomes she's toted here from The Archive. "I'm not going to talk to someone on the outside of the community about what's going on."

"But I'm supernatural too," Via insists.

Arletta flips one final page and hands the book across to Samantha before glancing back up at Via. "Yeah, so? You're not from the Hollow. By how green you look, I doubt you even knew about places like this until deciding to hang around her." Arletta nods to me. "And it's not like you can interview me for your podcast. I'm dead, remember?"

"But you're not dead," Via says.

"Wow, doll," Al says. "Nothing gets past you."

"Why are you dressed like that?" Via asks Arletta.

"That's how she always dresses," Samantha explains.

"Yes," I say. "It's ridiculous."

"Matilda," Arletta says. "Can you fuck off?"

"Well," I smirk, "aren't we in a good mood?"

Arletta flips me off just as Patrocles walks over and hands Via her glass of wine. "Matilda," he chides. "Don't harass my customers."

"Yeah, fangs," Al says with a taunting grin. "You're just grumpy because you're thirsting."

"That one seems thirsty." Arletta points at Via and Samantha laughs.

Via doesn't look amused. If she ends up having an immense distaste for Arletta as well, then I might like her even more.

"Can I get you something to drink, Arletta?" Patrocles asks, ignoring the snide comments being thrown back and forth.

"A riesling," Arletta says. "Thanks."

Patrocles nods and retreats back to the bar.

"Why did you let everyone think you're dead?" Via asks. "And before you mention the podcast, it's not like I'm going to record an episode saying I spoke to the undead Arletta Harrington in a secret, paranormal bar. That's not exactly the kind of story my producer, or anyone for that matter, is going to believe."

Arletta leans back and crosses her arms over her chest. "Why do you care?"

"Because you're a living dead girl." Via says this like it's obvious. "Everyone wonders what really happened to you."

"I'm not a living dead girl," Arletta snaps. "And I'm not undead either. I just went to a death realm for a few years."

Now Via looks truly flabbergasted.

I sigh, thoroughly exasperated by Arletta's flip-flopping dramatics.

"So the legends are true?" Via breathes. "About you and the Headless Horseman?"

Arletta narrows her gaze at Via but nods. "Yeah, they're true. Are you satisfied?" She picks up another book and begins to rifle through it while Samantha starts reading the one she's already holding.

"What's The Archive?" Via asks.

Arletta groans and slams the book shut. "Why are you here? Really?" She glances at me. "Did Matilda fill you in or something?"

"No." Via shakes her head. "She just invited me here. I didn't think it was anything other than a..." she glances at me, obviously unsure of how to continue. I wink. She betrays her poorly constructed icy demeanor with a small smile. "Samantha mentioned you were coming from The Archive but she didn't say your name."

Arletta looks at Samantha. "Why would you tell her that?"

"Because she's here and it's not a big deal. Who knows if Matilda was going to take her there next. It's like she said, she can't go make a podcast episode about all this. She already recorded a fake interview with me and Matilda earlier today, so it's fine." She glances at Via. "Right?"

Via nods. "Right."

Arletta sighs and slumps down a bit in her seat. "Fine, the seer can be in the know. The Archive is a library of different supernatural and paranormal texts that have been hidden away from the human world. Don't ask me why, that's way too long of an explanation."

"And it's hidden here in Sleepy Hollow?" Via asks.

Arletta shakes her head. "No, The Underground doesn't exist in Sleepy Hollow or anywhere, these halls and the establishments inside them exist in a space of their own, a thread in the fabric of the universe separated from the woven ones of non-magical folks' reality. There's a collection of doors across the globe that lead to The Underground and one of them happens to be in Sleepy Hollow. But who opened it first is anyone's guess." She shrugs then shoots a knowing smirk at Samantha.

Samantha chuckles like the two are in on some great inside joke. Knowing them, they probably are.

"The doors have to be opened by someone first?" Via asks. "Like, constructed?"

"Yes," Arletta says. "Any magical person can open them once they exist, but someone at some time in Sleepy Hollow's history had to open the door into existence."

"And you don't know who that is?" Via's brow quirks up. She's ever the quizzical one.

Arletta purses her lips, hiding an obvious taunting smile. "Nope."

Gods above and below she's maddening.

"But why were you in The Archive?" Via asks. "What are these for?" She gestures to the collection of books.

"Gods, you're nosy," Arletta says. "If you *must* know, we're researching how to kill Death."

"Um, what?"

Al and Samantha laugh, I bite back a chuckle myself, and Arletta smirks at Via, clearly pleased with the way she's shocked her.

"You can't kill Death," Via says.

"Wrong, seer. Let it hereby be known that I, Arletta Harrington, am going to kill the God of Death and replace him with a different man. A new deity for the realms here and beyond."

"Who?" Via asks.

Arletta grins deviously, the picture perfect image of the wicked witch everyone makes her out to be.

"The Headless Horseman, *obviously*."

Via's jaw is nearly to the floor when her cell phone rings. She suddenly looks embarrassed to be interrupted by a piece of modern technology. "Sorry," she mumbles. "Excuse me." The seer sets down her glass of wine and shuffles away from us, ducking into a corner to take the call. I watch her go, my eyes savoring the way her ass looks in those jeans.

Patrocles reappears with Arletta's wine. "What on earth are you four doing over here with that new girl? Everyone in the entire bar can sense the animosity."

Arletta takes a big gulp of her wine. "No animosity, Patrocles. We're just plotting the murder of Death."

"Oh," he says, uninterested. "That again? Well, good luck, Miss Harrington. I have absolutely no faith in you."

We all laugh as he walks away.

CHAPTER 8

WHEN YOUR PRIDE IS ON THE FLOOR, I'LL MAKE YOU BEG FOR MORE

OCTAVIA

"Where the hell are you?!" Rose screeches into the phone. "What's all that noise? Are you in a bar? Via, it's after four a.m.!"

I pull the phone back from my ear to look at the time. She's right. "Sorry, Rose, I got...distracted."

"By what? Why didn't you leave a note or wake me up or something? Jesus Christ, Via, I just woke up and you were gone!"

"I'm sorry." I glance behind me, Matilda is approaching. "I went out for a smoke and saw Matilda. She was headed to a bar and invited me along."

"You went to a bar with A VAMPIRE?!"

I hold the phone away from my ear. Even with the loud music all around me Rose's screeching still manages to rival its volume.

"Oh my god, yes, I did. She's...nice."

(She really isn't. Like, at all.)

The scent of Matilda's poppy perfume wafts over as she comes to stand right behind me. She runs her fingers through my hair, nails lightly scraping my scalp as she pushes the strands over my shoulder. A thrill thrums through my body and I feel an immediate ache for her, wishing she would put her fingers somewhere *else*.

"I'm going to head back now," I tell Rose. "I'm sorry I worried you."

Rose makes a sound halfway between a sigh and a growl. "Fine, you freak. Tell me all about your vampire date when you get home."

"Will do."

I hang up and turn around. Matilda's standing closer than I realize and I nearly stumble back from her. She moves in even closer, firmly pressing her hand to the small of my back.

"Let me walk you home, Via." Her tone is velvety and possessive. She's not even trying to enthrall me anymore. This might just be how she speaks to people. Or she might want to eat me. Hard to say. I should refuse her, but the red tint to her eyes tells me that's not really an option.

I tuck my phone away in my pocket and shimmy my arms into the sleeves of my coat. "Not like I have a choice. I have no idea how to get back to town from here."

Matilda smiles and takes my hand.

We leave the bar behind and make our way back through the winding tunnels until we reach the familiar door that leads back into the alley. I breathe in deep when we step outside, the cold night air assaulting my senses in the best way.

I turn around to face Matilda. "You knew Arletta was coming."

She pulls out a silver cigarette case, removing a slender

cigarette from inside (probably a Virginia Slim, she seems the type, I'm surprised she doesn't have a long cigarette holder like Holly Golightly), and placing it between her burgundy lips. "Of course I knew." She fishes out a lighter from inside her cape-like coat.

I watch as the tip of her cigarette ignites, a tiny puff of dragon's breath bursting into existence providing an extra glow to those lips I wish I didn't still desperately want to kiss.

She holds the still open case out to me. "Want one?"

I shake my head. I do, but I can't keep accepting things from her. Invitations to bars, cigarettes, intoxicating stares that make me want to take off all of my clothes.

She shrugs and tucks the case and lighter away. "What's the issue, dearie? You wanted to know the truth. Well, I gave it to you." She takes a drag from her pretentious, femme fatale cigarette and exhales the smoke in my face. "You're welcome."

"Why did you even come for me when I was a kid? I'm from Maryland, that's not exactly nearby."

Matilda leans back against the brick wall, the hidden door already having vanished with no trace that it was ever there.

"I wasn't always in Sleepy Hollow. I moved here a few years ago. Told everyone I *inherited* my house from my late aunt."

"Did you kill her? The woman whose house you took?"

Matilda laughs and takes another drag.

I swallow a grumble, I'm already fed up with her refusal to answer my more pressing questions. "So where were you before?" I try a different approach. "*Were* you in Maryland?"

"No, I was back in Slovenia for a bit. I'm from there originally." She flicks some of the ash onto the ground between us, narrowly missing my shoe. "The first ever vampires came from there. Or so Johan Weikkard Von Valvasor said."

"*Who?*"

She waves me off, puts her cigarette back between those damn lips.

"Then how did you come to me if you were in Slovenia? Where even is Slovenia? I didn't think that country still existed."

Matilda gives me what seems to be a disgusted look. I immediately realize I must have said something completely ignorant. My cheeks flush with embarrassment and the urge to pick my nails into bloody oblivion swoops down on me like a vulture.

"That's Yugoslavia, little seer. Slovenia is very much still around. It's in Eastern Europe at the intersection between the Alps, the Mediterranean, and the Balkans. And if you must know how I found a pretty little girl in Maryland, it's because you tried to summon me."

For the third time tonight, my heart turns to dynamite. When I was sixteen, I called out into the unknown for a friend to guide me. I was so lonely. Rose and I were going through a rough patch in our sisterly relationship, kids at school thought I was crazy, and I was still struggling to deal with the fact that everywhere I went I could see things other people couldn't: witches casting spells, ghosts lurking down hallways, demons creeping along dark streets, dogs that were really a shapeshifted human, fairies everyone else mistook for a trick of the light. It was tiresome and burdening. I thought if I could find a paranormal creature to be my friend (there weren't any in my school, I tried desperately to find one with no such luck) then life wouldn't be so agonizingly hard every day.

I knew I couldn't cast a spell, but I was good at research.

I ordered numerous books online and from neighboring library branches about the history of mediums and psychics to figure out how to reach out into the void that lay beyond this one. When I lit a circle of candles that fateful night years ago, perched by my open window with the screen carefully removed for optimal entryway to things that go bump in the night, I was hoping for a friendly ghost or a kind brownie.

What I got was a monster.

Even though Matilda stole my blood and my innocence that night, she didn't have the decency to take my loneliness with her. It plagued me, a sickness I couldn't escape, my very own death shroud. But I never dared try to summon an otherworldly friend again. I lived in fear for years that the vampire at the end of my bed would come back one day and take far more than just my blood.

After a while I tried to convince myself that Matilda was all in my head. A beautiful vampire didn't crawl up into my bed, straddle me, put a hand around my throat, and sink her fangs so deep into my chest that it felt like she pierced my heart. The scar on my chest was from something else. I climbed trees a lot as a kid. I played sports. I was clumsy. Maybe it was a birthmark.

I was drowning in maybes.

The older I got and the more of the hidden supernatural world I saw, the more I knew deep down that night hadn't been a dream.

But I never thought I would see her again.

Of all the gin joints in all the towns in all the world...

"I wasn't trying to summon *you*. I was trying to summon a friend."

Matilda finishes her cigarette and drops the butt to the ground, stubbing it out with her boot. She walks towards me until she has me backed up against the opposite wall. She places her hands down on either side of my head, her tall frame looming over mine, caging me in.

"I could be your friend."

I exhale softly, my glasses nearly fog up from how close she is, her breath hot on my skin (does she even *need* to breathe?). "You're not my friend."

Matilda smiles, but this time it's more vicious than any of her previous smirks or grins. This one is dark. This one is hungry. This is the smile that's haunted me for over a decade. She moves one hand away from the wall to pull back the collar of my coat, revealing my thin t-shirt underneath. She trails her fingers down until she reaches the collar of that too and pulls it aside to expose my chest. My heart. My mark. My tattooed memory. Her fingers skim across the scar, danger in the heat of her touch.

"You're right," Matilda breathes, leaning in as close as she can without letting her lips touch mine. "We're not friends."

She moves so fast I don't have time to process what she's doing until it's too late. I don't even see her fangs protrude from behind her human-looking teeth. I don't see her move her head down to my chest. I don't notice the familiar feel of her hand on my throat. I don't register that she has reopened my scar.

I cry out so softly my voice comes out strangled in the night air. My arms flail widely as I struggle for some semblance of stability amidst the pain. My head gets fuzzy and light as Matilda drinks my blood, her teeth sunken deep down under my skin. I whimper and let my hands move to the back of her head as the unfathomable, searing ache her mouth reaps upon me shifts slowly into the strangest, most beautiful kind of pleasurable pain I've ever felt.

My cries and whimpers turn to soft moans and mewls. Matilda finally releases my scarred heart to slide her bloody mouth across my collar bone and up my neck. She tenderly kisses my jaw and the corner of my mouth. I breathe in and out quickly, trying to regain my shattered composure.

"I—" I start.

Matilda ignores me and presses her hand between my legs, her palm flat against my core, providing enough pressure to create a sweet friction against the seam of my jeans.

"Fuck," I whisper.

Matilda moves her bloody lips to my ear and laughs before kissing my neck again. I don't feel her fangs anymore, but she still peppers softer bites and nips down the column of my throat while rubbing her hand back and forth against me.

"Please," I whine.

She laughs at my pitiful begging then swiftly unbuttons my jeans and slides her hand down past the barrier of my underwear, dragging her fingers through my wetness, pulling a pathetic sound from the back of my throat. I tangle my hands in her hair and bring her mouth down to mine. She doesn't resist me. It feels good to pretend that I'm at all in control. Her tongue dances against my teeth while she inserts two fingers inside me and begins to pump them back and forth, finger-fucking my cunt so hard that the unseemly, horribly human slapping sound her skin creates against my slick core battles for dominance against the sound of my moans.

"You look so pretty when you writhe, little seer." She kisses me again, taking my bottom lip between her teeth and digging in deep enough to make me whimper from the pain. "You bleed so beautifully."

She still has one hand on my throat as the other moves fiercely against my cunt, stealing any facade of being coy and composed around this beautiful monster.

"Kiss my heart," I whisper.

Matilda moves her mouth back to my scar, now torn apart and bleeding, the puncture wounds reawakened by the living memory. Matilda puts her beautiful, burgundy mouth to my skin, her lips press down over my heart—a vicious muscle. I cradle her head to my chest, keeping her close to me, savoring the feeling of her body pressed against mine as her fingers work between my thighs to undo me.

"Matilda," I whine again, hating how pathetic I sound.

Matilda laughs wickedly. "Do you want to come, dearie?"

I nod, breathless, feverish, *desperate*.

Matilda plants a final kiss over my bloody chest before removing her fingers from inside me and bringing them to her mouth. I gasp in horror at the absence of her hand, the denial of my orgasm dangling in the air between us. She still keeps her other hand around my throat, pinning me to the wall, making me watch as she sucks her sticky fingers in between her bloody lips. Multiple tastes of me must be mixing on her tongue.

"You're delicious, Via."

She squeezes my neck harder until I'm coughing and have to tap her arm to ask her to release me. She studies me for a second, fingers grazing up and down my skin. I want to beg her to put her fingers back inside my pussy and pull an orgasm from between my legs, but I know this is a game she's playing with me. Toying with her prey before she devours it. It's humiliating and addicting.

"Y–you," I start.

Matilda just smirks in that infuriatingly beautiful way that makes me want to punch her and drag her down into bed.

"Me?" she taunts.

"I thought…"

"Yes, dearie?"

She's so cruel and I can't bring myself to demand she make me come. If she wants to play this game of orgasm denial I'm certainly not going to be the one to keep begging for release. Judging by the flush in her cheeks and the smear of my blood across her mouth, I highly doubt I'm the only one who found pleasure in what just occurred.

"Did you leave any marks?" I ask instead of letting loose the begging at the back of my throat. She looks at me like I'm an adorable idiot. I roll my eyes. *This fucking vampire.* "I meant on my neck."

"No. I didn't choke you hard enough to bruise and I didn't use my fangs on your neck. Only here." She moves her fingers through the blood on my chest. "Only your heart. Like you wanted."

I roll my eyes again. "Pretty sure that's not what I said."

She shrugs. "Semantics. Shall I walk you home, seer?"

"The inn is right across the street and Rose might have a heart attack if she sees me with you."

Matilda laughs softly and readjusts my clothes to hide the bloody mess she's made of my heart.

CHAPTER 9

ONE NEED NOT
BE A CHAMBER
TO BE HAUNTED

OCTAVIA

Matilda is sitting behind the counter, a coffee mug in front of her, the tattered copy of *Wuthering Heights* hooked between her thumb and forefinger when I enter the bookshop the following morning, a chunky brown sweater covering any evidence of what her mouth did to me last night.

Rose hammered into me about my stupidity when I returned, but then a pain spell got the best of her and she downed a Coke, a Gatorade, and four ibuprofens before crawling back into bed. I haven't really slept. Just tossed and turned, but Matilda (of course) looks perfectly bright-eyed. The gift of the eternally nocturnal. I wonder if she has to sleep at all. There's still a lot of vampire lore I haven't been able to confirm or deny. She can walk in the daylight, this is obvious (even if she has to use an umbrella), I caught glimpses of her reflection in store windows when we all walked to her house yesterday, and she seems to be able to enter places without being invited. I have no idea though if she rests in a coffin, is put off by garlic, or can only be fully killed by decapitation.

None of these inquiries seem like appropriate topics for a second date.

Not that last night necessarily counts as a *first* date.

Matilda looks up from her book at the sound of the bell above the door. She smirks. "Morning, dearie. Sleep well?"

I approach the counter and rest my palms flat on the surface, steadying myself and my breathing. I rehearsed this a dozen times in my head since the sun rose, but I still feel an unease in my chest at the prospect of trying to be this confident in front of her.

"I think you owe me a meal."

Matilda raises an eyebrow. "Is that so?"

I tug the collar of my sweater down to reveal my scarred chest. "Or a drink."

Matilda smirks still, tilting her head slightly. "Alright, seer." She hops up from her perch, tucking a bookmark against the spine of her book, closing it and setting it aside, leaving Cathy and Heathcliff's fate unknown.

"Samantha!" Matilda calls out.

Samantha and Al emerge from one of the many aisles in the store. Samantha's brows furrow in annoyance when she sees me. I shift uncomfortably from foot to foot under her stare. I understand she hates my podcast, but her antagonistic nature is starting to feel a bit dramatic, all things considered. It's not like I'm the one who has a demon doing my evil bidding for me (not that I think Samantha is evil or that bad men like Peyton and Ethan don't deserve to be offed by a paranormal entity, but it's the principle of the thing).

"What?" Samantha sounds like a moody teenager.

"I'm stepping out for a bit, don't let Al destroy the place."

Al gasps and slaps a hand over his chest. "I'm hurt, fangs."

Matilda waves the demon off and strides over to me. She presses her palm to the small of my back and guides me out of the store. I let her keep guiding me like a lost lamb until we reach The Sentinel. I order a black coffee and Matilda orders tea (perplexing). We take up at a table in the back, Matilda runs a shiny, indigo-painted nail around the rim of her cup but never takes a sip. I guess she orders things for show. Blending in and all that.

"So, little seer, there's clearly something you want to know."

I take a sip of my scalding coffee and try to ignore the way it burns my tongue. "I just...want to know about *you*."

"And why is that?"

I try to mentally shake off how oddly hurtful I find the question. I thought we had some kind of connection. For gods' sake, I apparently summoned her as a child and last night in the alley...well that was certainly *something*. Surely she feels it too.

"Don't you want to know about me too?" I ask. "After all this time?"

Matilda remains statue-still in her chair. I fleetingly think of the *Twilight* series and then remind myself how foolish that is. Out of all the vampire lore I've consumed over the years, I highly doubt any of Ms. Meyer's is going to ring true. I've yet to see Matilda sparkle in the sun or climb a tree like a spider monkey.

"All right then." Her fingers circle her cup again, the tea untouched. "Why don't you and your sister look anything alike?"

Well, that's a weird place to start.

"We're adopted."

"Is she Irish?" Matilda asks.

Now, I'm the one to smirk. "Are you asking because of her red hair? She's a white American, don't they all claim to be part Irish?"

Matilda remains silent. I sigh at my joke. It didn't stick the landing so much as crash into a pile of dust. My body is fighting like hell not to descend into panic mode, my brain at the ready to over analyze every single second of this interaction.

"It's not like she's done a DNA test or anything, I'm sure she's more than just Irish, most white Americans are, but her birth last name is O'Malley, so she leans into the Irish heritage thing. She likes to party hard on St. Patrick's Day." This is not an exaggeration, Rose loves that holiday.

"She changed her last name?"

"Our Ma changed our name to hers when she adopted us. Majestic. I like it, we're a family."

Matilda smiles, circles her mug again. "Your Ma might have some Slovenian in her."

"What?"

"Majestic is an Americanized version of the Slovenian and Croatian last name Majetič. Did she speak of vampires often?"

"Not everything in my entire life has been about you."

Matilda laughs. It seems nothing I say, nor how irked I get can deter her or put her ill at ease.

"And where is your Ma now?" she asks.

Bees buzz inside my lungs preventing me from getting a full breath. I wish she hadn't asked about my family.

"She's dead," I say, fighting to keep my breathing even. "Cervical cancer. A few years ago."

Matilda stares at me for a moment. I anticipate the usual sympathetic gaze and hollow 'I'm so sorry' that always follows this declaration, but Matilda just shrugs and twirls her finger around her un-sipped tea again. "Pity."

She gets a drop of tea on the tip of her finger and stares at it contemplatively, almost as if she's wishing she could lick her skin clean. I wonder if she misses food and drink too terribly? But as quickly as the look came over her, it's gone again. She wipes her fingers on a napkin before settling her gaze back on me.

"And what about you? Where does your ancestral family hail from?"

I'm not sure if I'm annoyed or relieved by her apathy. "Puerto Rico. But, like many adopted kids, I don't know anything about my birth parents and I've never really cared to. My Ma *was* my mother and Rose *is* my sister. I love them and I don't need anyone else. Our Ma chose me and Rose and we chose her right back. Do you hail from some long lost era where such a concept is foreign to you? Get with the times, baby."

I feel proud of myself for being bold enough to address Matilda by a pet name. I can't help but smile with my eyes over the rim of my coffee mug as I take a less scalding sip and Matilda smirks at my sass.

"Is that your way of asking how old I am, dearie?"

I put my mug back down and shrug. "Take it how you want."

"I lost count many birthdays back."

"When did you die?"

Her fingers circle her cup again. I wish they'd circle something else.

"Sometime during the 16th century I think."

"Did you choose this?" I had meant to save that question for a more intimate moment, perhaps when we trusted each other more, but my obsessive need to know gets the best of me and pulls itself free from my lips too soon.

Matilda actually looks uncomfortable for once. "In a way."

"What does that—"

"I need to get back to work. Thank you for the company." She gets up and walks around the table, stopping by my side to cup my chin in her hand. "Be careful where you lurk alone at night, little seer. Not every creature is as nice as me."

She licks her teeth, I catch a glimpse of her fangs. She releases me and leaves.

CHAPTER 10

YOU CAN'T LOVE ANYONE CAUSE THAT WOULD MEAN YOU HAD A HEART

MATILDA

"Why do you keep hanging around with the podcaster?" Samantha asks, leaning across the counter.

I turn the final page of my book before answering her. "Because I feel like it. Why do you keep hanging around with Arletta?"

"Because she's my best friend."

I set the book aside and roll my eyes. My pain is acting up, causing Samantha to irritate me more than usual. My left leg is cluttered with painful bumps of tense muscle I'll have to massage out later, biting back cries. Blood would help ease the agony, but the fatigue of my suffering will make it hard to focus on hunting and I doubt Patrocles has gotten any more real stuff in stock over the last twenty-four hours. Drinking from Via last night helped quell the worst of the burning spasms that wove throughout my back and into my hips and thighs, but the sweetness of the partial relief has worn off.

I glance over at Samantha, eyeing the tendons of her neck. The sweet sound of her coursing blood sings to me. Even a sip from her throat would help dull the ache in my muscles. It probably wouldn't be as strong or as savory as the blood of that pitiful creature called Via, but it could temporarily sate me nonetheless.

I glare at Al for the millionth time. Goddamn demon messing up the frequency of my blood supply. He'd surely try to stake me through the heart if I tried to drink from his little gothic lover.

"I can handle closing," I tell Samantha, ignoring her petulant look. "Why don't you head home to your *best friend.*"

She sighs. "Why do you hate her?"

Because she's beautiful and powerful and gets everything she wants.

"I find her tiresome. Which is also what I'm soon going to find you to be if you don't stop pushing me."

"I swear since you dyed your hair black your heart followed suit."

I laugh. "Witch, my heart turned black centuries ago."

SANDY IS HAUNTING my halls when I get home. I hang my umbrella on a rack by the door and take off my books before ascending the stairs to find him lurking outside my bedroom.

"Don't you have any other friends?" I chastise, passing him and heading into the room, sitting down on the edge of my four poster bed.

I reach for a jar of CBD cream Samantha gifted me after Samhain and begin to roll down my stockings so I can apply generous amounts to my knees in a futile attempt to stave off the worst of the inflammation.

The specter follows me inside. "Don't *you?*" he taunts. "That seer and you seemed to be rather cozy last night."

I scoff. "She was a lovely meal. Nothing more." I finish rubbing in the cream and debate taking some painkillers. Consuming anything but blood often leads to any vampire feeling ill. It's become a weekly war inside my mind if I want to tolerate nausea in return to dulling the pain or face the pain full on to avoid the nausea.

Without even the pain flare to spur on my constant hunger, the familiar thirst that is only natural to my kind claws up my throat, sinking into my tongue like sand. My belly is full of burning coals, my throat is lined with shards of glass, and the spasms in my muscles are heightening these typical sensations to hellish levels.

Sandy gives me a look that conveys he thinks I'm full of it, but he has far too much decorum to ever speak such an accusation aloud.

"There are men coming to the Hollow," he says. "I've seen them in the witch's dreams."

I don't need to ask which witch he means. There's only one in town with a strong enough prophetic power to predict such a thing.

"More podcasters?"

My tone is vexed, he refuses to indulge it, remaining poetically stoic and serious.

"Monster hunters."

I groan and flop back on the bed. "This year is so annoying," I lament.

Sandy comes over and lays down beside me. "I concur."

CHAPTER II

PEOPLE DYING IN THEIR BEDS WHILE CLUTCHING GHOSTLY CONFESSORS

OCTAVIA

Rose sleeps soundly beside me. Her pain flare is still acting up, so she downed two glasses of wine after sending off an email to Arnold with the notes for our Dullahan episode. I'm starting to doubt if we've gathered nearly enough content, but Rose has assured me we can fill in the blanks of Sleepy Hollow related content with research from around the world.

Specifically Ireland.

Oh, the irony.

I lay in the dark and scroll through my notes app for this episode. I jotted down several things to research before we left for this ill-fated trip and promptly forgot to follow up on any of them once I got swept up in the whirlwind of Matilda's orbit. Now one name in particular stands out to me.

Chrom Dubh.

I open a new internet tab and type the name into the search engine. A wealth of information pops up. I start to read through article after article and by three a.m. (figures), I've realized something vital. Something that will make even Samantha and her stupid demon see value in me.

I know how Arletta Harrington can kill Death.

I look over at a slumbering Rose and contemplate waking her up to tell her about this development. I will first have to inform her that Arletta is alive and fill her in on all the details I left out last night when I got home from my little paranormal excursion. My sister is going to be so pissed about how much I censored my story, but I just didn't have the energy to get into all of it. Now something in my gut tells me darkness is coming to Sleepy Hollow and none of us, magic and magic adjacent, will be safe unless Death is on our side and perhaps Arletta is correct that the only way to do that is to make sure the God is someone we can trust.

She didn't explicitly say that's *why* she's doing it. Wanting to move her undead boyfriend up in the ranks of the harbinger of doom ladder probably has quite a bit to do with it, but still.

I start to reach out to shake Rose's shoulder when a distant, echoing voice distracts me, pulling my attention to the window. I see a figure drifting through the drapes. I fumble in the darkness for my glasses, sliding them up my nose to bring the blurry being into focus.

I almost laugh at the sight.

Matilda smiles wickedly as she emerges from the polyester fabric covering the dingy window of this pitiful excuse for a hotel room.

"Come to me, Via."

I sit up in bed, swinging my legs over the side to face her. "Okay, Nosferatu, tone it down."

"Nosferatu wasn't the vampire's name, it was Count Orlok."

"He was also a half rotting corpse, so the similarities are pretty limited."

Matilda's mischievous grin remains plastered across her face. "Are you coming or not, little seer?"

I lean a bit closer to her, taking in the somewhat misty nature of her demeanor. She's coming to me now almost as an apparition. I add astral projection to my mental catalog of true vampire lore.

I stand up and take a step closer to her, "Come where?"

"My bed."

She winks at her own double entendre and then vanishes into the night, her body seeming to become one with the moonlight itself. I glance back over my shoulder at my sister's sleeping form and know she's going to be mad at me when she wakes up in the morning to find me gone again, but the damn gay panic and overwhelming lust inside me has burrowed so deep in my bones that I can't ignore it anymore. My vampiress has called and I must answer. I snatch one of our notebooks from our bags of podcasting equipment and scribble a hasty note out to Rose then grab my Converse and coat before racing out the door into the unknown, devil may come.

Oh, I mean *whatever* may come.

I KNOCK on the door to Matilda's comically gothic house but no one answers. I try the handle and find that it's unlocked. I guess she doesn't have much to fear from intruders. Even if she does sleep at night it's not like we live in an era rife with vampire hunters breaking down the doors of mysterious maidens.

I step inside the foyer just as Matilda waltzes down the upstairs hallway clad in a floor-length black silk robe that clings to her frame in all the right places. My mouth practically salivates at the sight. She splays her hands out across the bannister and smiles that tantalizing smile down at me.

"Good evening, little seer. Didn't anyone ever warn you about going into dangerous places alone, late at night?"

I tilt my head, rolling my lips to keep from outright biting them, and toe off my sneakers. "Maybe I like a little danger."

Matilda chuckles. "You, a vanilla little thing, like danger?"

I head to the stairs and begin to slowly climb, keeping my eyes glued to hers.

"I'm not *so* vanilla."

Matilda raises an amused brow. "Aren't you?"

This time I can't resist the urge to bite my lip as I give my head the slightest, almost taunting shake. Matilda doesn't say anything more, just keeps her gaze locked on mine until I've finished climbing the stairs and come to stand before her.

"I'm not so young and innocent anymore," I tell her, tilting my head back to be able to meet her penetrating stare.

"Well then." She purses her perfect lips and subtly jerks her head in the direction of a large set of ornately crafted doors that must lead to her bedroom. "Follow me, dearie."

Matilda turns and heads off to her room, I trail behind like the lovesick puppy I am. Not that I'm in *love* with her. More like in lust, infatuation, in like...entranced? Something. But you can't fall in love with an otherworldly being of darkness you met once.

And saying we 'met' when I was a teenager is definitely a stretch, it's not like there were any formal greetings or introductions. Just my swallowed scream and the violence of her embrace. A perfectly painful penetration that's haunted me ever since. The knowledge that I'm about to feel so much more than just her teeth or even her quickly thrusted fingers in the darkness of a dirty alley has my heart racing so fast it could potentially be a health concern.

Matilda throws open the doors to her room, leading me inside. The place is lit by dozens of candles and the bed is draped in red satin blankets. This woman is ridiculous. It's incredible.

Matilda turns to face me, strides across the small swath of space between us, and slips my glasses off before I can protest. She folds them up neatly and sets them on a nearby chest of drawers that looks like it fell out of a fairytale. She stalks back over to me and reaches out to drag her fingers across my shoulder. Even with the bulky fabric of my sweater between us, her touch electrifies me.

"Take this off," she commands, pinching at the fabric.

I do as she says without hesitation, my usual anxious state washing away in the wake of my excitement. Matilda stands back and watches me tug my sweater up and over my head, tossing it aside on the floor. She takes in the sight of me bare from the waist up, save for my black bra.

My scar is visible in the candlelight.

Matilda smiles demurely and steps in closer, coming into focus for my blurry eyes. She trails a long, lithe finger down my jaw until she reaches my chin and tilts my head back slightly.

"Stay close to me," I breathe. "I can't see you clearly if you don't."

"Don't worry, little seer. I have no intention of going far. You're mine for the night."

I'll be yours forever is the first thought that flits through my brain as she runs the fingers of her other hand through my hair. She tugs hard and sharp, the pain stinging across my scalp, making me hiss, but I don't pull away. I know she can't control me the way she could control a regular human, but I don't need her vampiric enchantment to go weak in the knees from her touch. My practically uncontrollable desire for her is taking care of that just fine.

Matilda leans in close, her frame pressing up against mine as one hand tugs at my hair and the other holds my head in place. "Kiss me," I whisper.

Matilda chuckles softly in amusement but she takes pity on me. She leans down and presses her wine-stained lips to mine and the entire universe stands still. It's cliche and trite and ridiculous but every other kiss in the world suddenly pales in comparison to the sensation of Matilda's mouth on mine. Even the kisses she and I have shared prior to this point are a dull gray contrasted with this kiss's screaming color.

I part my lips and let her tongue invade my mouth, savoring the citrus and smoky taste of her. She slides the hand gripping my chin along my jaw and up into my hair to join the other. My hands instinctively reach out and hold onto her forearms, keeping her close to me. Even with my eyes closed I want her as near as can be, I want our forms to crash together, to blend into one beautiful, passionate painting of a body experiencing euphoric bliss. Surely Matilda must feel the fire between us as fiercely as I do. Why else would she have come to my room tonight—

seeking me out in my bed for the second time in my life? That can't just mean nothing.

We *can't* just be nothing.

Matilda begins to drag her fingers from my hair, along my jaw, and down my neck, her nails scraping across the surface of my scar. I inhale softly, already drunk off her touch.

"Matilda," I whine.

"I know what you need, dearie."

Matilda slides one hand around the back of my neck and grips it firmly, the pads of her fingers pressing down hard into my flesh. I gasp again from the slight pain of her touches. I've never had much experience with pain in the bedroom, but the idea of it always intrigued me and now the reality of it is better than anything I ever could've dreamed. My mind flits back to how it felt the times her fangs tore into me and the disturbingly sweet ecstasy that quickly chased the pain of the puncture. I want to feel it again and I want her to be fucking me while it happens.

Matilda, sensing my need, uses her grip on my neck to drag me over to her large, four-poster bed. She shoves me hard and I gasp, throwing my hands out in front of me to catch myself against one of the posts, my chest heaving. Matilda's barely done anything to me yet and I'm already so turned on I can feel a slickness soaking into my underwear and my nipples hardening against the confines of my bra. If Matilda doesn't put her hands back on me soon, I think I might go mad.

I hear her laugh again from behind me, a bit more taunting this time. It irks me, but not enough to call her out on it, not right now when I'm half dressed and all but begging her to ravage me. She pushes my hair over one shoulder and plants her lips on my skin, letting her teeth gently scrape the surface without ever fully digging in. I'm sure she'll bite me, it's in her nature and I'm not naive enough to fail to realize how inherently erotic the act of drinking blood is. For fuck's sake, she drank from my breast the other night, my neck would be amateur hour in comparison.

Matilda keeps one hand pressed against my shoulder as she trails the other down my spine until it reaches the clasp of my bra, which she undoes easily. She uses my hair as a lever to tug me back so I can release my hold on the post and let my bra slide down my arms and onto the floor.

"Turn around," Matilda commands. "Let me see you."

I do as she says, resting my back against the post, gazing into her enchanting eyes. She smiles and traces her fingers along my jaw. "Aren't you just perfect."

Then she drops to her knees before me and reaches for the button of my jeans.

"I—" I gasp, so surprised by her sudden movement. It's not that I want her to stop, but if just kissing my mouth and neck undoes me so severely, I can hardly imagine what her mouth on my cunt is going to do.

Destroy me, probably.

I do my best to maintain my balance as Matilda tugs my jeans down and off. She does the same with my socks, smirking at the little TARDIS design on them. Then her violent hands are at my damp panties and she wastes no time in doing away with those too. I inhale sharply, nervously. The anticipation is a knife buried in my chest as I await her lips. But she takes me by surprise and plunges two fingers deep into my core, drawing a pathetic whimper from deep in my body. The vampire keeps her eyes on me as she begins to fuck me with her fingers, her pace steady and unforgiving. Just when I'm about to beg for her to put her mouth on me, she lunges forward and does just that. She flicks her tongue across my clit as her fingers pump harder and I cry out. With her free hand she uses her unnatural strength to push me sideways and back onto the bed where I land with a bounce. The sudden absence of her tongue and fingers makes me want to weep, but Matilda doesn't leave me wanting for long. She quickly climbs up my naked form and plants a bruising kiss against my mouth, shoving her tongue between my teeth and letting me taste myself.

I bite down on her tongue, wishing I had teeth sharp enough to pierce, drink down her blood and make it my own, but the monstrous nature in this bedroom is solely hers and I am resigned to lay back and take what she deigns to give. This ancient, damn near ethereal being is sharing her bed with me. It's still hard to wrap my head around. The fact that she's now trailing her kisses and teeth and tongue back down my body until she reaches my cunt and begins to suck and bite my clit isn't helping the matter of trying to process all of this in a healthy way.

Rose will argue that none of this is healthy.

Letting a vampire fuck you isn't healthy. Especially when that vampire lowkey assaulted you when you were a teenager and is also clearly not much of a girls' girl (this is a cardinal sin in my sister's book). But I can't bring myself to care about what's healthy or logical or right with Matilda's tongue in my pussy.

She reaches a hand up to pinch one of my nipples, hard enough that it makes me writhe, unintentionally grinding against her face, but she doesn't seem to care. In fact, she seems to take it as an invitation be even more aggressive, using her other hand to resume the finger fucking. She alternates between my breasts, pinching and squeezing, her tongue flicking against my clit, stopping to suck and bite every few swipes, and her fingers pounding into me. It's too much, my orgasm is building from this trifecta of stimulation and I come with a scream, spasming against her tongue and hand, tears welling up in the corner of my eyes. But she doesn't stop, she removes her tongue and releases my breast. Her other hand's fingers stay buried inside me as she trails her lips across my mound over to my inner thigh. The hand that was on my breast presses down on my pelvis, pinning me to the bed.

"What are you—" I start.

Matilda sinks her fangs down into the soft flesh of my inner thigh while fingering me to a second orgasm and the pain turns maddening as it mixes with the pleasure. I try to arch my back and writhe away from the terrible pressure of her fangs but she keeps me still, utilizing that inhuman strength again. I think I say 'no' or 'stop' or maybe I just moan and get lost in the pain. Maybe I should've insisted she ask before biting me, or maybe I should just be grateful she didn't bite my breast again, seeing as last night's mark is still healing.

Matilda keeps drinking from me, the ugly slurping sounds echoing around the room as she drains me. I fleetingly worry she's going to kill me and that this is going to be the stupidest autopsy ever, but then she finally frees my flesh and starts to fuck me harder until I'm a writhing, screaming mess against her. Bleeding and coming, covering her in different bodily fluids that she seems to savor.

This is filthy and vile and brutal and far too erotic to be normal.

But I've never been normal, have I? Getting bitten and screwed by this beast of the shadows is just what I needed to allow myself to finally embrace the parts of me I've tried to suppress my entire life. The parts that were too weird or dark or questionable. Here in Matilda's bed, my come and blood all over her mouth, her eyes searing into mine, I finally feel at peace.

She crawls back up the bed and kisses me with her bloody mouth, the scent of sex heavy in the air.

"Perfect, dearie," she murmurs against my mouth. "Just perfect."

CHAPTER 12

ERE THE BAT HATH FLOWN

MATILDA

"Will you tell me how you became a vampire?" Via asks.

I look across at her. We're laying side by side, facing each other, I've been absentmindedly twirling her dark hair around my finger for who knows how long and she's been looking up at me with those puppy love eyes that with many past lovers I would have found sickening but on her I must admit is a bit endearing.

"It's a boring story," I say. "There was a man, he promised me something impossible and I believed him."

Her brows furrow together creating a little crease. She looks cute when she's being serious (which is honestly a bit too often for my taste).

"Is that it?" she asks.

"My apologies I don't have a more torrid tale to tell."

She rolls her eyes, I flick her chin with my forefinger, and she smirks.

"What did he promise you?"

I fight back the urge to sigh in annoyance. It is a habit I've acquired from centuries of mortal lovers longing to unravel all of my secrets, collecting them like trophies to display proudly as if they've made some great achievement by getting my tongue in their cunt. Poor dears never seem to realize that there's been troves of men and women just like them that came before and there will be troves more to come after. My ability to fall in love died along with my beating heart. That is the curse of eternity, but also the freedom I never possessed when I was alive.

Choice.

"A cure," I answer her. "To my pain."

"What pain?"

"I don't know what it's called. There weren't names for such things back then. You were just considered weak, sickly, prone to fatigue." I wave my hand blithely in the air, not in the mood to start talking like a Jane Austen character. I chose my current surname after Carmilla Karnstein after all, not Fanny Price. "But I imagine whatever ailment I have is similar to whatever plagues your sister."

I see her brow crease smooth in surprise. I laugh.

"I've lived long enough to be able to recognize when a woman is in pain. It wasn't hard to figure it out. What with the cane and the way she seems to always be cringing. Does she have a name for it?"

"Cervical spondylosis. Neck arthritis. It affects her spine and her joints. You might have similar symptoms to Rose," Via continues. "Do you get dizzy a lot and feel faint? Or really fatigued and get tension headaches? Or joint pain and—"

"I don't need you to diagnose me," I tell her, an edge to my voice. I had enough of healers and quack doctors when I was alive, I don't need to hear the modernized spiel from a human.

"Right, duh." Via shakes her head against the pillow. "Vampirism cured it, right? I mean you're...not alive anymore so..."

"It did not cure it," I tell her. "But it made it easier to manage."

"How so?"

"Blood."

A silence hangs between us for a moment. It's odd and I don't exactly know what to make of it. I scan her eyes for an answer and find only emptiness. My Via, who is usually the epitome of an open book, has suddenly become closed off from me.

"Blood helps with the pain?"

Is she being dense on purpose?

"Yes," I answer, annoyance dripping back into my voice. "It's a better remedy than any modern medicine or old midwife practice. It dulls the pain to a more tolerable level than anything did when I was alive or any painkiller can now. Besides, I can't really stand modern painkillers, consuming anything but blood makes me feel ill. Blood is the best medicine. The man from my past didn't cure me by killing me but he did unknowingly give me the gift of freeing me from the bonds of my circumstances."

I expect her to continue with her trail of questions, this time shifting to what exactly my poor, pitiful circumstances were as a woman in the 16th century. I try to find some patience, but I've already shared more with her than I have with anyone in centuries and the whole ordeal has me feeling rather annoyed.

Via sits up, clutching the sheet to her chest. "Blood

helps with your pain and there's a blood shortage at The Back Room."

She doesn't phrase it as a question. I sit up beside her, making no attempts to cover myself with the sheet. I push her hair back over her shoulder and run my fingers through it.

"Nothing gets past you, dearie," I tease.

But Via doesn't smirk or roll her eyes or react in any way I've come to expect from her. Instead she scurries out of the bed and starts to get dressed, frantically collecting her discarded clothing.

"What are you doing?" I demand, getting up and reaching for my robe.

She spins around to face me. "Are we anything?" She's almost dressed again, holding her ugly sweater in her shaking hands. I can make out tears in her eyes. "Do I mean *anything* to you?"

I don't dignify her ridiculous inquiry with a response.

She huffs and tugs the sweater over her head. I stand by my bed and watch as she struggles to re-don the monstrosity and then locate her glasses on the chest of drawers. Once her vision is clear again, she glowers at me. Despite her attempt at toughness I can see the flush spreading across her cheeks and creeping down her lovely neck (I will bite there next). Her hands shake, her eyes seem hazy, almost like she's high. Her silly anxiety is consuming her. I would almost find it laughable if it wasn't directed at me. Her emotions are strong and heady and disgusting. It's one thing to have her swooning and fawning over me, it's another to have to face her immaturely misplaced ire.

"You just invited me over here so you could drink my blood, didn't you?" Via's cheeks are cherry red now. "And last night, in the alley, were you just having a pain flare?"

I sigh and lean against the bedpost. "Would you like me to feel remorse for being what I am? So I find you to be a more delicious dinner than some drunk idiot wandering around at this hour, don't act like that's such a great offense to your honor."

Via balks at me. "So what, I should take it as a compliment? I'm just something to consume? I'm nothing more than...than *medicine?*" She steps closer to me. She's shaking but still trying to appear tough and undaunted. It's almost cute. "You drank from Peyton and Ethan too, didn't you? You knew they were horrible men and you didn't care if you hurt Arletta and Samantha by keeping them around."

I laugh. I can't help it anymore. She looks so absurd, glaring and behaving as if her mere mortal being holds any superiority over my eternal existence.

"You caught me, oh great seer."

She scoffs and shakes her head. "You don't love me," she whispers.

"I am not a thing to love or be loved, you idiot girl. Do you really think I have regrets for killing and drinking? Do you want me to feign sorrow and repentance for you? Is that what it takes to shut you up?" I close out the space between us, forcing her to tilt her head back to be able to hold my stare. "I'm so sorry, Octavia," I coo and taunt. "I can be good, teach me how to be a good little vampire, won't you?" I grin wickedly with the final words and Via's tears finally slip past her lashes.

"You're evil," she whispers.

"Of course I am. You've read your fairytales, seer. I'm a beast, a creature of the night, a blood-thirsty monster. Did I really fuck you so good that you forgot that?"

Via's mouth drops open in shock. She moves away from me, reaching for the doorknob.

"Do you love me, little seer? Did you think it was fate that brought you here to the Hollow—to my bookstore? That we're soulmates destined across the stars? Is that the story you told yourself?" I close in on her, practically pinning her against the door. "Did you think you were so special to me all because I crawled into your bed a few years ago?" I laugh again. "Poor dearie, you really thought you were the only lonely maiden I consumed? Poor, sad, little seer. How pathetic your loneliness has made you."

"Shut the fuck up!"

Via screeches, trying to push me back and failing to do so—she's no match for my strength, but I smirk at the attempt nonetheless.

"You're not better or smarter or cooler than me." She's shaking now, her hands curling into fists by her sides. "You're a walking corpse that has to live off blood. You're the one who was stupid enough to believe some strange guy had a miracle cure to chronic pain. You think surviving horrible things gives you a pass to be horrible to others? News flash, Dracula, you're not the only one who's suffered. You're not the only person walking this earth who's had sad and traumatic and awful shit happen to them. You think you're special because you're a vampire? This is Sleepy Fucking Hollow. I'm a seer, I run into a different paranormal being on every other block, and believe me, you're nowhere near the most powerful one I've seen."

She storms out and races downstairs. I trail after her, not bothering to exert my super speed, her legs are short, it doesn't take long for me to reach the landing as she tugs her shoes on below.

"You can see our power, dearie? Is that what you're telling me?" I want her to be lying. She *must* be lying.

"Yeah." She tugs on her second shoe and heads for the

front door. "And like I said, you're not the most powerful creature in town, not by a long shot."

She *can't* be telling the truth. I won't allow this to be the truth. I did not live this long to not be the strongest one in the room.

"Oh really?" I ask, rolling my eyes. "Then who is?"

Via smirks and opens the door. "Arletta Harrington."

This time it's my jaw that drops and Via who laughs, the sound echoing even once she's slammed the door behind her.

CHAPTER 13

AS TO THAT MATTER, I DON'T BELIEVE ONE HALF OF IT MYSELF

OCTAVIA

The blood inside my skull is going to boil, my brain is the frog, only all too aware of the rising temperature. The world shifts around me, the road tilts beneath my feet, sending me sprawling to the concrete sidewalk, tearing a hole in the one of the knees of my jeans, scraping my skin, painting me red with blood. I can't breathe. I'm too hot. My face, my ears, my neck, my throat, my chest.

Thank the gods no one is out this late, this far on the outskirts of town where the wicked witches live, to see me curling into a ball, spiraling into madness, here on the sidewalk under a judgmental moon.

I press my hands to my cheeks, hoping my chilled, shaking palms will cool down my burning skin. Nothing smells right, I have earmuffs on that I can't seem to get off. I am in a cocoon, a coffin. I am dying. Matilda drank me dry.

I managed to keep it together long enough to tell her off. In that moment, I felt stronger than I have in a long time, even if my insides were catching fire as each word left my mouth.

I blink through tears and look at the bitchy moon above me but it's fuzzy, even with my glasses on. The world is TV static. I can't feel the sidewalk beneath me anymore. I exist in a suspended state of unfounded terror. I'm so dizzy. The planet is spinning without me, leaving me behind in an abyss of fear.

I'm sweating. My pores leaking sour-scented terror.

I'm going to vomit. Expel toxic fluids all over the streets of this cursed town.

I'm dying.

Let me disappear. I can't live like this. I can't.

I manage to dig my phone out of my coat pocket. I pull up Rose's contact and consider calling her, asking her to come get me, but I don't want to wake her. I don't want to burden her with my panic attack. I barely even want her to know how I've been spending my evening. I close out of my contacts and open my calming app instead. I manage to steady my shaking hand enough to tap the START button and a computerized voice spills out of my phone:

PANIC ATTACKS ARE NOT DANGEROUS. The voice chimes. *PANIC ATTACKS ARE TERRIFYING BUT THEY ARE NOT DANGEROUS. THEY ARE NOT FOREVER. LET THE ANXIETY FLOW THROUGH YOU. STEADY YOUR BREATH-ING. BREATHE IN FOR FOUR, HOLD FOR FOUR, EXHALE FOR FOUR, EMPTY FOR FOUR.*

I try to follow the voice's instructions and do the five senses grounding exercise my therapist has drilled into my head, but dammit my heart yearns for the Xanax bottle in my suitcase back at the inn.

<u>Five things I can see:</u>
1 The sidewalk beneath me.
2 The bitchy moon above me.
3 Stars. So many stars.
4 The edge of my glasses frames.
5 My chipped nail polish.

<u>Four things I can hear:</u>
1 My breath.
2 My racing heartbeat.
3 An owl hooting somewhere in the distance.
4 A car whizzing by far away.

<u>Three things I can touch:</u>
1 The cold sidewalk.
2 My bulky coat.
3 My bloody knee.

<u>Two things I can smell:</u>
1 My sweat mixing in with my deodorant and the scent of
Matilda's sheets.
2 My dry shampoo.

<u>One thing I can taste:</u>
1 The ghost of smoke from Matilda's kiss.

THE APP IS STILL CHIRPING at me. My breathing is still a bit too
shallow. I don't know for sure how long I've laid here, but
the panic is finally starting to pass. Slowly, like a river
meeting the sea. I manage to sit up. I can't be that far from
where I need to go. I don't know which is less safe: walking
alone at night or getting into a rideshare alone at night

when the only person in town I'm sharing a location with is asleep.

But I made it to the fucking vampire's house alive.

I can make it to the witches'.

I close out the calming app, silencing the robotic voice. I open up Maps and type in walking directions.

THIS IS PROBABLY A REALLY stupid idea.

As if to emphasize my point of doubt in this decision, the wind chooses this exact moment to howl. I close my eyes and sigh. I take out my phone and check the time. It's almost five a.m. This is an obnoxiously early time to be knocking on a witch's door, but, like I said, stupid idea.

It can't be much dumber than climbing into Matilda's bed.

Right?

Before I can triple guess myself, I raise my fist and knock.

The door creaks open and nothing could have prepared me for the sight before me. Standing there on the other side is the Headless Horseman.

He. Is. So. *Tall.* If I had to tilt my head back to look at Matilda, I practically develop a crick in my neck looking at him. He's dressed in a colonial outfit, and where a head should be, a flaming Jack-O-Lantern rests.

Hello, little seer.

The carved mouth of the pumpkin doesn't move, but I hear his deep voice inside my mind, like he's telepathically transmitting his words directly into my brain. I take a nervous step back and nearly fall off the front porch.

"H–hi," I stammer.

I almost can't believe it. The legends are true. Not just of The Headless Horseman himself, but the legends of Arletta Harrington as well. That crazy witch really did run away to a mythical realm and fall in love with an honest to goodness dullahan.

"Is Arletta here?" My voices comes out wobbly and pathetic.

"Hesse!"

Arletta screeches from behind him, but he's so damn big I can't even see her tiny frame around his bulking one.

I hear her feet stomping over and then her head of wild brown hair peeking out from around the Hessian. "You can't answer the door! Are you insane?"

It was only the seer, the Headless Horseman—*Hesse,* apparently—think-speaks to her.

Arletta rolls her eyes. "I was in the bathroom when she knocked, you couldn't give me two minutes?"

She already knows of my existence, what does it matter if she sees me?

Watching a five foot tall witch who looks like she got dressed at Spirit Halloween arguing with an over seven foot tall headless creature of myth like they're an old married couple is definitely making the top ten on list of weirdest things I've ever experienced in my life.

Arletta groans then finally looks at me. "Octavia, what are you doing here? It's five in the morning. How did you even get my address?"

Now I'm the one who wants to roll their eyes. Arletta's house shows up on countless online listicles of most haunted places to visit in Sleepy Hollow, not to mention Samantha has business cards for her herbal witch side hustle sitting on the front counter at the bookstore. It didn't exactly take extensive sleuthing to locate her address.

"I know how you can kill Death," I tell her.

Arletta's mouth opens in surprise. Hesse's pumpkin mouth doesn't, but that was expected.

The witch steps back and gestures to the living room behind her. "You better come in."

I step into the infamous witch's house and take in her tiny living room, cluttered with half-melted candles, old books stacked all over the place, incense burning in various holders, an assortment of potted plants nestled by the window, and weird gothic artwork hung up on every wall. The room is crowded. Maybe Arletta and Samantha aren't used to having to share the space. I wonder if Hesse sleeps and if so *where?* I glance at the small velvet green couch against the wall. I don't think it would fit him.

"Sit down," Arletta says. "Do you want some coffee or something?"

I sit down on the old couch and nod. "Yeah. Black's good."

"Weirdo," Arletta mutters before wandering off to the kitchen, leaving me alone with Hesse.

The Headless Freaking Horseman.

He just stands there and looms over me, staring down at me with his pumpkin eyes.

"Soooo..." I can't stand the silence. I'm usually moderately okay with a relatively comfortable silence, but the fact that I'm in the house of a witch with a terrifyingly powerful aura who doesn't really like me that much and her undead harbinger of doom boyfriend is using his gourd head to stare into my soul, it's hard to feel comfortable with any second of the quiet. My normal resting level of anxiety begins to amp up until my insides feel like they're spinning. I'm going to go insane if I don't fill the air between us with words. I try to swallow the growing lump in my throat and ask: "Your name's Hesse?"

It is now. Once it was something else.

"Ooookaaay," I say slowly. "How long have you been back in Sleepy Hollow?"

Since this past Samhain.

It's only a few weeks out from Thanksgiving so he hasn't been here long. I guess the lore that he can only cross over on Halloween night must be accurate, otherwise I imagine he and Arletta would've come back a lot sooner, especially since Samantha and Arletta are besties.

Arletta saves me from drowning in the agonizing awkwardness when she re-emerges from the kitchen carrying two mugs of coffee. She hands me my dark, inky one while hers is so light it seems like it's made up of more cream than coffee. She sits down next to me, takes a sip without blowing to cool it down (she's insane in so many ways), and holds my gaze with her intense stare.

"So," she says after swallowing the scalding sip. "How do we kill Death?"

"You need to go to Ireland and find Crom Cruach."

Arletta and Hesse stare at me.

Well...Hesse doesn't exactly stare...it just *feels* like he does.

Then Arletta laughs. Once. A sharp, barking sound. I'm starting to see how some people might find her off-putting. But I have to admit, she would probably be more predisposed to like me if I didn't come here to try and expose all of her secrets.

"I'm sorry," Arletta starts. "We have to do what?"

I sigh and stare briefly at my black coffee, then take a big gulp for courage, ignoring the burn as it goes down my throat. "I think Hesse is a dullahan. One of the many headless harbingers of Death."

I am, Hesse agrees. *Death granted me this form to return to the Hollow for vengeance.*

"Do you have to be beheaded in life to be a dullahan in death?" I ask.

Hesse is quiet for a moment.

I never thought about it. I have never met the other dullahans. Death does not like his creations to mingle with one another too frequently. The Realm beyond this one can be rather lonely.

He and Arletta share a look that seems almost pained. How tormentingly isolated he must have felt all those years until Arletta came along.

But, Hesse continues. *My kind of undead beings are everywhere, different Holy days allow them to cross the Veil back into the Realm of the living to wreak havoc. My Holy day is Samhain, but there are others, it always depends on how they died and what they died for.*

"Wow, Hesse," Arletta says. "Thanks for the lore drop. Why didn't you tell me any of this before?"

It did not seem relevant.

Arletta groans and slumps back against the couch. "Fucking men," she mutters. "So, who's Crom Cruach?" she asks me. "That sounds Gaelic. I'm German, not super familiar with that flavor of folklore. Neither is Samantha."

"Crom Cruach is Crom Dubh's older brother."

"And Crom Dubh is?"

"Well..." I glance between her and Hesse. "I think Crom Dubh is Death."

"You *think?*"

I nod and fish my phone out of my pocket. I set my barely touched coffee down on the end table and pull up the article I was reading. I pass my phone to Arletta who takes it with a skeptical gaze.

"Crom Cruach was killed years ago by St. Patrick, then his younger brother Crom Dubh took his place. Death went from being a natural part of life to something that could be toyed and tampered with. Sure, most people still die randomly and by the chance of it all, but some deaths are controlled and planned; the deaths the dullahans doll out."

Arletta is silent as her eyes flick back and forth reading the words on my phone screen. I decide to continue on with my rehearsed speech before she's sick of listening to me.

"Crom Cruach's soul might still be in the Realm of The Dead, the Underworld, the Beyond—whatever you call it. If you go to his altar in Ireland and make a sacrifice to summon him then he might be willing to help you take out Crom Dubh and install Hesse as the new God of Death."

Arletta finally looks up from my phone.

"Octavia," she says. "This is a Wikipedia article."

"Wow, Arletta," Al says, appearing in the living room. "All those weeks you've been shut up in The Archive with those stuffy, old tomes, and little Miss I-See-Dead-People found the answer in one night in a Wikipedia article."

Arletta practically *growls* at the demon.

"It's not a Wikipedia article," I insist.

The three paranormal beings look at me. My cheeks flush in anxiety and embarrassment.

"I mean...it's a Wiki page, but..."

"It sounds right to me," Samantha says, walking out of the hallway at the back of the house to stand beside Al. "But you're the diviner, Arletta. What do you see?"

"This isn't an episode of *That's So Raven*," Arletta snaps. "I don't just get visions in the blink of an eye. I need to scry."

Al dramatically gestures to a small door near the back of the living room that I didn't notice until now. "Then by all means, all great and terrible Arletta Harrginton, go scry and reap the secrets of what the future holds so we can start planning our road trip to the land of the lucky."

I exhale slowly, sinking deeper in the couch, deciding now isn't a good time to tell them all that I've seen the truth of Arletta's power.

The witch glances at me, her eyes flickering with the glimmer of a taunting smirk.

She's much more than just a diviner.

She's a sorceress.

If anyone can summon a dead God, it's her.

CHAPTER 14

EVERYONE IS A BOOK OF BLOOD; WHEREVER WE'RE OPENED, WE'RE RED

MATILDA

It's hard not to hate Octavia Majestic. An insufferable woman.

I stand by the window and watch her stumble down the road, shaking and breathing heavily. It's pitiful and stomach churning. Why can't humans ever maintain any semblance of composure when overcome with their ugly emotions?

Did I ever behave in such a way when I was alive? Surely not.

At least the girl's blood quelled my pain flare long enough to plan who to kill next to drink and then decant until The Back Room replenishes its supply of the real thing.

I feel like I'd been staked.

Long after Octavia is out of sight I lay on my bed, watching the sunrise behind my curtains. I was so wrapped up in the seer last night I forgot to pull my blackout curtains closed. The sun beats down on me, feeling sickening. I loathe sun fatigue. I get enough of it at work whenever Samantha decides it's too dreary in the shop and throws the blinds open, ushering in the ghastly rays of warmth.

I still can't believe Samantha never replaced my umbrella after that time she lost it cavorting around the cemetery with Albatross.

Why must mortal women be so unbearable?

I touch my lips. The taste of Via's blood and come still slick on my tongue.

Fuck her.

Damn her.

I never should have crawled into her bed all those years ago.

Thanks to Sandy ambushing me later this morning to deliver another ominous warning about the supposed monster hunters he senses through various peoples' dreams, I'm twenty minutes late to work. Samantha is sitting behind the counter in my usual spot when I walk in, the stupid demon floating behind her. She looks up from the old spell book she's reading and shoots me a perturbed look.

"Tardiness is unbecoming, Miss Sheridan."

I flip her off. She laughs and closes the book. "Tell me, Matilda, do you have any idea who showed up on my doorstep this morning at an ungodly hour?"

No. There is absolutely no way.

Samantha smirks, Al laughs. My horror must be painted plainly across my face.

"That's right, your girlfriend stopped by."

I try to remain stoic as I come around the counter and deposit my purse beneath the register. "She's not my girl-friend. What was she doing there?"

"She figured out how to kill Death," the demon says with a laugh as he somersaults through the air.

I straighten up and set my sights back on Samantha and Al. They're both so ridiculous.

"Is Arletta still on about that?" I ask.

Samantha's amused expression melts away. A familiar look of exasperation takes its place. "Is she still *on about it* as of forty-eight hours ago? Yes, she is. And I'm going to help her."

"It's your funeral." I step around her and head through the beaded curtains into my office.

Samantha trails behind me.

"Why did you chase Octavia away? You clearly like her."

I stop in my tracks, nails biting into the skin of my palms. "You don't know what you're talking about. Drop it."

The herbalist circles around me, determination woven throughout every muscle of her small frame. "All these years you've been alive and you've never been in love? Never wanted to be?"

I sigh. I'm weary of mortals nagging me about such trivial things.

"Let me guess," she continues. "You loved someone once and they betrayed you and now you've decided to swear off of it for all eternity. Was it the person who turned you?"

"My sire was not my lover. Best to leave the divining to Arletta, *herbalist*." I spit her title like a slur. It's no secret that many supernatural beings consider herbalists to be one of the weakest forms of magic practitioners.

Samantha doesn't take the bait, she continues on, unmoved by my admittedly weak attempt at an insult. "You may not want to tell me when you died but—"

"Do I look dead to you, little witch?" I bite out, but she ignores me and continues on.

"I'm sure you've been around for a while, otherwise you probably wouldn't have picked such a classic fake last name."

"*Samantha*—" my voice has morphed into something akin to a snarl.

"But you can't spend forever alone. What's so wrong about letting yourself love that podcaster? Granted she's really annoying but Albatross is annoying too and—"

"I do not love."

"Oh, I forgot," she says sarcastically. "The Big Bad Bloodthirsty Creature of The Night is above such things. Whether it's love or passion or just like-minded company, no one is meant to be alone, Matilda. No one."

"I'm not alone. I have you."

A look of surprise shows in her eyes. "Yeah. You do have me." She gives me a small smile but it vanishes after only a moment. "But I *am* going to help Arletta and Hesse kill Death."

I huff. "What does that have to do with anything?"

"Death is the old Celtic God, Crom Dubh. We need to summon his older brother, Crom Cruach to help us destroy him. And to do that we have to go to his altar in Ireland."

Whatever I might have been expecting her to say, that wasn't it. "Excuse me?"

She nods and moves past me to head back out through the beaded curtain. "We leave in two days, so unless you want to be all alone in this store, your big creepy house, *and* at The Back Room, I suggest you go chase down your podcaster paramour and apologize for whatever the hell you said to her last night that left her with red eyes on my porch this morning."

CHAPTER 15

THE LIVING AND THE DEAD, CAN THEY CO-EXIST?

OCTAVIA

I shuffle back into the inn at six in the morning, Rose is sitting on the bed reading Dramione fanfiction on her phone and icing her neck down from a bout of inflammation. She shoots up when I walk through the door, hugs me, and then slaps my shoulder.

"You're insane! First you go to a vampire's house and then a witch's? Were any other reckless stops made during your night out that my phone didn't pick up on location share?"

"Yeah I visited the troll under the bridge."

She rolls her eyes then picks up her purse and finally opts to use her walker. "We need to go to The Sentinel. I have a bitch of a tension headache forming. I need french fries and a large coke—*badly*."

"Oh my god," I try to reach for her arm to steady her but she shifts away, always insistent on her independence. "Did you have a bad spasm? Did you fall?"

She shakes her head and begins to wheel her walker to

the door. "No, but I'm going to at some point soon if I don't get some caffeine and sugar in me. Let's go."

We head outside, call an Uber, struggle a bit to fit her walker in the trunk, and head off to the 24-hour diner that has quickly become our favorite haunt in this town over our brief time here.

We sit at a suspiciously sticky table in the corner. Rose continues to intently read her fanfic as we wait to place our order. I twirl my hair anxiously and play back the entire interaction with Matilda in my head. I feel like such a fool, a timeworn, predictable character in a pulpy gothic novel. It's embarrassing. I need to tell Rose about the dullahan of it all and the whole killing Death theory I cooked up. We might be able to weave it in a way that works for our episode.

"So are we going to talk about it?" Rose asks.

I manage to sit up, my head still spinning. "About what?"

Rose huffs. "Don't play dumb. We need to talk about how you've spent a decent portion of this work trip flirting with an evil vampire."

My hands clasp in my lap. An already butchered pinky nail begs to be clawed at. "Matilda isn't evil."

"Does she kill people?"

I shrug. "I don't know."

Rose narrows her gaze. "Liar."

I shrug again. "She's a vampire. They need blood to survive. We don't even need meat to survive and we eat it. You ordered a bacon burger the other day."

"That is hardly the same and you know it. I don't go stalking cows in the middle of the night and drinking their blood while they writhe in pain, fully *alive*."

"That's an absurd analogy."

"*I'm* not the one being absurd," Rose insists. "You are!

You're sneaking out, going places alone, not telling me, leaving me behind! We came here together to complete this project *together*. And you've been ditching me to go hook up with some psychotic creature of darkness."

"That's not fair," I mumble. I glance down at my hands. My pinky nail is bleeding.

"Are you in love with her?" Rose demands.

I look back at my sister, surprised by the earnestness in her stare. "I hardly know her."

Rose sighs, almost sounding defeated. "I don't buy that. There's something you're keeping from me. You've never been into hookup culture and are always telling me you can't be with anyone physically if you aren't feeling an emotional connection to them. You told me she can't compel you or enthrall you or whatever the supernatural term for her creepy persuasion powers is, so that means you genuinely care about her. Have you met her before? Before this trip?"

I don't say anything. My ring finger nail is bleeding now too.

"When?" My sister knows how to take my silence for an answer.

"A long time ago." I smear the blood on my torn jeans.

"Did you know she was going to be here when we planned this episode?"

I shake my head. "I never even knew her name before we saw her in the bookstore for the first time."

"And yet you love her."

I can't take this anymore. I slump down in the booth, tugging a napkin from the dispenser and begin to fold it into an origami heart. "Read your fanfic," I mutter.

Rose groans, fed up with my behavior, but I can't bring myself to care right now.

My sister pulls her giant purse out of the basket of her walker, digging through it until she produces a Bandaid and ointment for my knee. She slides them across the table to me without saying anything. I mumble a 'thank you' before uncapping the ointment and spreading it liberally across my scrapped kneecap.

"Fuck!" Rose says, tapping furiously on her phone.

"What is it?" I ask.

"Arnold emailed me, the network just axed *Spook Street*."

The floor tilts, pushing me to the precipice of the abyss of panic once more. My cheeks flush, my hands shake. I might as well peel off my fingernails now and let the blood flow freely.

"*What*? Can they do that? They can't do that, right?"

Rose continues to tap away on her phone, brows furrowed, eyes blazing. "Apparently there's some loophole in our contract and we haven't gotten enough listeners to validate travel costs, blah, blah, blah, corporate bullshit."

I go still and let her words wash over me. As I make sense of her sentences, my head falls against the table with a loud *thunk* at the same time a voice says: "You ladies ready to order?"

The same beautiful waitress who's served us every time we've come in stands over the table, giving us a skeptical look.

"Yeah," I mumble. "Black coffee."

"Large coke with light ice and lots of french fries," Rose adds. "And two slices of whatever pie is your favorite."

The waitress smiles and laughs softly as she scribbles it all down on her pad. The bells and charms in her hair jingle a happy tune as she moves her head with each chuckle. I look for a name tag, but she's not wearing one.

"I'm Rose," my sister says, seemingly reading my mind (as sisters are prone to do). "This is my sister, Via."

The waitress nods. "Yeah I've seen you two hanging around here." She narrows in on me. "Don't tell me you're all bent out of shape because of the vampire at the bookstore."

Both mine and Rose's jaws drop. The waitress just laughs.

"Don't let that old hag get you down, her heart's as black as the night." She laughs again at our gobsmacked expressions. "I'm Melody, by the way. Melody Lakes."

"So...you've...been in Sleepy Hollow a long time?" Rose says tentatively. "Since you know all about..." Rose waves her hand in the air to encompass the whole of paranormal beings roaming the streets.

Melody nods. "Born and raised. The Sentinel has been in my family for generations."

I lift my head up from the table. "Are you the current owner?"

"Technically my Gran's the owner, but her Chronic Fatigue Syndrome says otherwise." Melody glances at Rose's walker, the silent question in her eyes.

"Cervical Spondylosis," Rose answers.

Melody nods. "That's rough. I'll get your order right up. Mind the vampires." She winks, but there's a strange sadness behind the gesture.

We watch her go in silent awe.

"This town is so much weirder than I ever imagined," Rose says.

I nod as I slump back in my seat, my body just doesn't seem to want to hold itself upright for very long today.

"What should we do?" she asks. "Without the podcast we're unemployed."

I shrug. "Maybe we could strike out on our own. Lots of podcasts are indie."

Rose gives me an exasperated look. "With what funding?"

"We could get sponsors."

"Who? Your rich vampire girlfriend?"

I glare at her.

Rose realizes her overstepping and raises her hands to placate my silent rage.

She starts tapping away on her phone again. "Our bus leaves tomorrow morning, once we're back in Maryland we'll figure something out. We may not own the copyright to *Spook Street*, but it's not like our well of ideas is dry. It also looks like we'll still get to release the dullahan episode and collect the royalties, so there's that. After it drops and our contract officially ends, we can start pitching around and go back to shitty hourly jobs to keep the lights on until another network picks us up."

Her voice wavers on the last part.

We both look at her walker.

Neither of us dares speak the quiet part out loud, we just wait for our food.

CHAPTER 16

YOU MUST COME WITH ME, LOVING ME; TO DEATH

MATILDA

"This is a good idea," Sandy says as he materializes beside me in the pouring rain.

He's opted to forego his more humanoid form tonight and as a result he's a black, swirling, monstrous mass of a being. I'm sure to many the visage is quite terrifying, but I stopped fearing monsters on the night I became one myself.

I don't acknowledge Sandy's remark. I do not want his praise, nor do I want to know what kind of lurking he's been up to today to know what my plans are. I grip my umbrella tighter and continue to march down the sidewalk. The moonlight streaks through the pouring rain, basking Sandy's darkness with an otherworldly, celestial-like glimmer.

"It's good to see you happy, old friend," he says.

I stop and look over at The Sandman, offering him a piqued expression. "Is this what happiness looks like?"

His razor-sharp teeth glint against his shadows as he smiles. "On you? Yes."

He disappears into sparkling dust. I sigh and head to the little inn where Via and Rose have been renting a room. I'm about to cross the street and head around the side to where their window is nestled when the familiar smell of cigarette smoke beckons to me from down the alley where the door to The Underground hides.

I head into the alley to see Via sitting on the ground with her back up against the bricks. She's soaked, her hair plastered across her face, the lenses of her glasses covered in raindrops. If it weren't for the tiny, cherry-red glow of her cigarette, one could easily mistake her for a large rat creeping about. I take an unnecessary deep breath and walk over to her, keeping my footsteps silent and swift. Via doesn't notice my presence until I'm standing a foot away, my umbrella stretched out to shield us both from the rain.

Via tilts her head up slowly. She drops her cigarette to the ground and uses a damp sleeve to smear the raindrops across her glasses.

I glance at her discarded cigarette, the tip sputtering out in the water. "You know smoking kills."

The corner of Via's mouth perks up the tiniest bit in an almost smile. "Yeah. Well, so do you."

I fight the unnatural urge to smile back. I do not blush or swoon or long for things or people, especially mortals. But gods above and below, if there isn't something about this woman who has called out to me through the years.

"Samantha said you're leaving tomorrow," I say.

Via nods. "Our bus leaves at ten a.m."

I nod too for some reason.

It practically kills me all over again, yet I manage to

drag the words up from inside me and pull them free from my throat.

"I think you should stay."

Via's brows furrow and her chest heaves, her collar bones poking out from beneath that ridiculous sweater.

"What?" she breathes.

Damn her.

"I...would *like* it if you stayed. With me." Suddenly I'm as foolish as a teenager again and I can't seem to stop the words falling from my lips faster than the raindrops around us. "Samantha told me what you told her and Arletta about Death. They're all leaving for Ireland in a few days, and I can't run my shop alone and I don't know if Maryland is the best location for podcasting but perhaps you could do that silly podcast here and...be with...be with *me*."

Via is silent.

I'm an idiot.

I hate that I care. I *loathe* that I care. She's just some stupid mortal girl who happens to be able to see ghosts and witches and vampires and the like. What should it matter if she wants me as badly as I unfortunately want her?

Just when I think I'm going to go mad from her lack of response, she stands up, grabs my face in her hands and pulls my mouth down to hers. In an instant I open my mouth to deepen the kiss, letting the umbrella blow away as I hold onto her face as well. The wind blows and the rain pours and the taste of her mouth is the sweetest flavor I've tasted in all the centuries I've been alive.

When we finally break apart, Via lowers her heels back down to the ground. I hadn't even realized she was on tip-toe, she's so very tiny. She rests her forehead over my cold, dead heart, and takes a deep breath, like her lungs can't seem to get enough air, my kiss has stolen it all.

"I love you too," she whispers.

Fucking hell, this godsdamn mortal.

I kiss her again, pushing her body up against the bricks as I tangle my hands in her soaked hair. The rain mixes in with our sweat and spit, creating a slick coat to our skin, our clothes clinging to us in the bitter November night. I can't get enough of her, my hands reach for her neck, her breasts, her hips, her cunt. I work one hand under her sweater to tease at her nipple while the other tears at the button and zipper of her wet jeans. It's a bit more of a struggle than I have the patience for, but eventually I'm able to run my fingers down her slit, feeling the wetness already pooling between her thighs. She moans into my mouth and I drink the sound down greedily. I tug her hair hard, tilting her head to the side, exposing her neck. I don't bite her, even though I want to so badly. I can't even remember the last time I had sex without drinking my lover's blood. I haven't fucked another vampire in decades and they're the only creature I don't drink from. Some vampires share blood, but I've never cared for the taste and it provides no actual sustenance. I never saw the point. But just like her spit, Via's blood is the most decadent I've ever had.

"It's okay," she whispers. "You can bite me."

I pull back for a moment and look into her eyes. She smiles. "You are not just a meal to me," I tell her. "You are more than medicine."

She smirks. "That's as close to an apology as you can do, huh?"

She laughs, raindrops falling onto her tongue. I lean forward and suck the pink muscle into my mouth, drinking the storm. She moans and writhes against me while I slip two fingers into her cunt and spread them wide, pressing against her inner walls until I reach the spots that make her squirm.

"Fucking hell, Matilda," she moans. "Do it. Do it now."

I twist my fingers as I crook them forward, Via moans louder. I clamp a hand down over her mouth and dig my fangs into her neck. She lets a muffled scream loose against my palm while her body twitches beneath the hand I have pressed to her pussy. Her fingers dig into my back, she writhes and wiggles and comes hard. I drink her screams and her blood in tandem. The combination of the two, coupled with the feeling of her pretty pussy clenching around my fingers as I milk her dry is the most euphoric I have felt with a lover in a long, long time.

I release her neck but continue to fuck her through to a second orgasm until she's a weeping, shaking mess in my arms.

"See how well you take me, dearie?" I whisper in her ear, my fingers pumping furiously inside her. I add a third one, determined to fuck her until she can barely stand. My wrist cramps, my fingers spasm inside her but I fight to disassociate from the pain. I want to feel her clench around my fingers more than I want to ease my pain. She can help me ice my joints later. Right now I want to consume her, heart, soul, bones and all. "You were made for me, little seer. You've been mine all these years."

"Yes," she gasps against my lips. "Yours."

I pump harder then pull my fingers free and flick her clit until she's coming with a scream like the good girl she is.

When the aftershocks begin to leave her body and her bones can finally be still, I kiss her forehead and wrap her up in my arms.

Via won't always be this young. She will wither and age. One day she will waste away in my arms, leaving me to walk this earth alone once more. Her short mortal life will pass before me like days. But they are days I don't want to miss.

Maybe I can no longer love.

Maybe my heart is nothing but a withered, black mess.

But I know one thing for certain: I can never be sated in any sense of the word without Octavia Majestic at my side.

EPILOGUE

MELODY

"Word on the street is that Arletta Harrington is alive," my Gran says, looking up from her knitting long enough to raise a bemused brow.

I laugh and twist my hair up into a top knot before tying my apron around my waist to get ready to open for the day. Gran is sitting in her favorite chair behind the counter, a dime back romance novel in her lap, the rainbow scarf she's knitting in her hands. She's promised to learn the new touch screen register today, but I know she's just saying that as an excuse to sit down here with me as I do the early morning prep.

The Sentinel used to be a 24-Hour Diner, but now we're more of a As Close To 24-Hours As We Can Manage Diner. Our hours are never consistent on any given day and we always stay closed for a few hours while the sun is down so I can get enough sleep to function when the five a.m. early bird breakfast rush tends to start.

"Anyone with a drop of magical blood in their veins knows that girl is alive, Gran." I grab a rag and wipe down the counter. "The real gossip is that she's fled to Ireland with Samantha Waverly Kos in tow."

"Now why would a sweet girl like Samantha go and do something like that?" Gran asks.

I shrug and begin to wipe the counter. "Who knows, witches are crazy. But rumor has it Arletta's leading a little band of paranormal creatures on a special mission."

The clicking sound of Gran's knitting needles ceases. "And what mission is that?"

I glance over my shoulder at her and smirk. "To kill Death."

~

OLE LUKØIE (AKA LUK)

I pace back and forth in my study. Well, really for me it's more floating than pacing, but still. I can't stop thinking about what I've seen in the nightmares of so many minds here in the Hollow and all across this side of the country.

One nightmare breaks up the endless barrage of peril yet to come.

A woman with braids in her hair dreaming the dream of a memory about a brother who bled out beneath a vampire's fangs.

Oh Matilda, you old fool.

She should have left when she had the chance.

The Monster Hunters are here.

SCARY LANE PODCAST EP. 1: GAY VAMPIRES AND
WHERE TO FIND THEM(transcript excerpt)

OCTAVIA:
Hello, ghouls! I'm Octavia Majestic.

ROSE:
And I'm Rose Majestic. And you're listening
to the inaugural episode of our new
podcast!

OCTAVIA:
You might know us from our former podcast
'Spook Street' which was hosted on our old
network.

ROSE:
That we totaaaalllyyyyy amicably parted
with.

OCTAVIA:
wheeze

ROSE:
But now we're going at it solo! Or,
well, duo.

OCTAVIA:
Independently. So that means you folks
might have to listen to some annoying ads
and shameless promos for our Patreon.

ROSE:

Speaking of! Before we get into the topic of today's episode, we'd like to take a moment to thank the first sponsor of this new podcasting endeavor: 'The Raven's Quill'.

OCTAVIA:

If you're ever in Sleepy Hollow—

ROSE:

Which you should be, it's great here.

OCTAVIA:

—make sure to visit 'The Raven's Quill' for all your spooky, bookish needs. Now, onto the show topic at hand! Rose, tell me: have you ever read the book *Carmilla* by Joseph Sheridan LeFanu?

ROSE:

The one where she gets staked and beheaded at the end when they find her sleeping in a coffin of the blood of her victims?

OCTAVIA:
Jeez, spoiler alert.

ARLETTA, HESSE, SAMANTHA, ALBATROSS, MATILDA, OCTAVIA, ROSE, MELODY, AND LUK WILL RETURN IN BOOK 4: SWOONING FOR THE SANDMAN

133

ACKNOWLEDGMENTS

As always, first and foremost, thank you to Marcia Ruiz-Olguín (@mar.s.cottageofdreams on Instagram). Without you I would not have the courage to sail the Starless Sea and breathe the haunted air. My stories also wouldn't be what they are without your much needed and appreciated feedback. Thank you for listening to every endless string of voice notes where I asked how Matilda could "Be more evil."

Thank you to my sister for proofreading even though you prefer spooks to romance, and for helping talk me down from late night spirals, and watching objectively terrible horror movies with me. Thank you for advising me on how to portray Via's anxiety disorder in an accurate and respectful manner. And thank you for attending author events with me and helping me when my chronic pain gets bad.

Thank you to my parents for putting up with me, believing in me, and supporting me. And thank you especially to my mom for helping me with my chronic pain at any hour of the day.

Thank you to Jay Gaunt from TheAwkwardBookworm on YouTube. You were the first person I ever shared my writing with and your feedback, love, and encouragement has been so dearly appreciated all these years.

Thank you to my Instagram hype team: Mika (@_mikasreadingcorner_), Amanda Nikole (@amandas.-bookcorner), Ali (@thatsmutgirl), and Fern (@fern.does.-books). You four have helped ease the stress of marketing and book promo and just been all around wonderful lights of positivity and joy.

Thank you to Karolyn Haines, aka @palettepriestssart on Instagram, for creating beautiful cover art and character art, and always being down to help me with my spooky, spicy visions.

Thank you to Bianca D. Kay, aka @bianca.auth on TikTok & Instagram, and Mal Burns, aka @spookyxmal on Instagram, for always being wonderful and supportive friends as well as cheering me on in my creative endeavors.

Thank you to YOU, the readers. I never imagined a silly little novella about a snarky witch getting with the Headless Horseman would become a #1 Amazon Bestseller and spawn an entire shared universe of spooky, spicy romances. Arletta and Hesse's love story has changed my life and it's all because of the love you all have shown to them. Thank you, thank you, thank you from the bottom of my heart.

ABOUT THE AUTHOR

Molly Likovich is the #1 Amazon Bestselling Author of *Riding The Headless Horseman*. Her writing has appeared in numerous literary magazines and anthologies including *Rust + Moth, The New Mexico Review,* and *Love Letters to Poe Vol. 3*. She has a B.A. in Creative Writing and considers herself an unofficial Beetlejuice Scholar. When she's not writing she can be found haunting the nearest cemetery or re-watching classic Barbie films. Learn more at molly-likovich.com and follow her on TikTok, Instagram & YouTube @magicalmolly

ALSO BY MOLLY LIKOVICH

SEXY SLEEPY HOLLOW SERIES

Riding The Headless Horseman (#1)

Smashing Pumpkins (#1.5)

Romanced by The Headless Horseman (#1.75)

Getting With The Ghoul (#2)

THE FAOINSGEUL WOODS DUET

Not a Myth (#1)

The Willow's Silence (#2)

STAND-ALONES

Send in The Clowns

There's Something in The Woods

Loved Alone

Be Terrible

Falling for Jack Frost

The Firefighter Before Christmas

FANFICTION

Lumos & Lattes (Dramione)